The Soft Machine

Other Works by William S. Burroughs
Published by Grove Press

Naked Lunch
The Ticket That Exploded
Nova Express
The Wild Boys

William S. Burroughs

The Soft Machine

GROVE PRESS □ New York

Grove Press
841 Broadway
New York, NY 10003

The Soft Machine appeared in the collection *The Soft Machine, Nova Express, and The Wild Boys: Three Novels*, published as a Black Cat Book in 1980 and an Evergreen Book in 1988.

Library of Congress Cataloging-in-Publication Data

Burroughs, William S., 1914–
The soft machine / William S. Burroughs.—1st ed.
p. cm.
ISBN 0-8021-3329-0
I. Title.
PS3552.U75S6 1992
813'.54—dc20 92-18811
CIP

Manufactured in the United States of America

First Edition 1966

First Black Cat Edition 1967

First Evergreen Edition 1992

CONTENTS

THE SOFT MACHINE

Dead on Arrival

I WAS WORKING the hole with the sailor and we did not do bad. Fifteen cents on an average night boosting the afternoons and short-timing the dawn we made out from the land of the free. But I was running out of veins. I went over to the counter for another cup of coffee. . .in Joe's Lunch Room drinking coffee with a napkin under the cup which is said to be the mark of someone who does a lot of sitting in cafeterias and lunchrooms. . . Waiting on the man. . . "What can we do?" Nick said to me once in his dead junky whisper. "They know we'll wait. . ." Yes, they know we'll wait. . .

There is a boy sitting at the counter thin-faced kid his eyes all pupil. I see he is hooked and sick. Familiar face maybe from the pool hall where I scored for tea sometime. Somewhere in grey strata of subways all-night cafeterias rooming house flesh. His eyes flickered the question. I nodded toward my booth. He carried his coffee over and sat down opposite me.

The croaker lives out Long Island. . . light yen sleep waking up for stops. Change. Start. Everything sharp and clear. Antennae of TV suck the sky. The clock jumped the way time will after four P.M.

"The Man is three hours late. You got the bread?"

"I got three cents."

"Nothing less than a nickel. These double papers he claims." I looked at his face. Good looking. "Say kid I known an Old Auntie Croaker right for you like a Major . . . Take the phone. I don't want him to rumble my voice."

About this time I meet this Italian tailor cum pusher I know from Lexington and he gives me a good buy on H. . . At least it was good at first but all the time shorter and shorter. . . "Short Count Tony" we call him. . .

Out of junk in East St. Louis sick dawn he threw himself across the washbasin pressing his stomach against the cool porcelain. I draped myself over his body laughing. His shorts dissolved in rectal mucus and carbolic soap. summer dawn smells from a vacant lot.

"I'll wait here. . . Don't want him to rumble me. . ."

Made it five times under the shower that day soapy bubbles of egg flesh seismic tremors split by fissure spurts of jissom. . .

I made the street, everything sharp and clear like

after rain. See Sid in a booth reading a paper his face like yellow ivory in the sunlight. I handed him two nickels under the table. Pushing in a small way to keep up The Habit: INVADE. DAMAGE. OCCUPY. Young faces in blue alcohol flame.

"And use that alcohol. You fucking can't wait hungry junkies all the time black up my spoons. That's all I need for Pen Indef the fuzz rumbles a black spoon in my trap." The old junky spiel. Junk hooks falling.

"Shoot your way to freedom kid."

Trace a line of goose pimples up the thin young arm. Slide the needle in and push the bulb watching the junk hit him all over. Move right in with the shit and suck junk through all the hungry young cells.

There is a boy sitting like your body. I see he is a hook. I drape myself over him from the pool hall. Draped myself over his cafeteria and his shorts dissolved in strata of subways. . .and all house flesh. . . toward the booth. . .down opposite me. . . The Man I Italian tailor. . . I know bread. "Me a good buy on H."

"You're quitting? Well I hope you make it, kid. May I fall down and be paralyzed if I don't mean it. . . You gotta friend in me. A real friend and if."

Well the traffic builds up and boosters falling in with jackets shirts and ties, kids with a radio torn from the living car trailing tubes and wires, lush-workers flash rings and wrist watches falling in sick all hours. I had the janitor cooled, an old rummy, but it couldn't last with that crowd.

"Say you're looking great kid. Now do yourself a

favor and stay off. I been getting some really great shit lately. Remember that brown shit sorta yellow like snuff cooks up brown and clear. . ."

Junky in east bath room. . . invisible and persistent dream body. . . familiar face maybe. . . scored for some time or body. . .in that grey smell of rectal mucus. . . night cafeterias and junky room dawn smells. three hours from Lexington made it five times. . . soapy egg flesh. . .

"These double papers he claims of withdrawal."

"Well I thought you was quitting. . ."

"I can't make it."

"Imposible quitar eso."

Got up and fixed in the sick dawn flutes of Ramadan.

"William tu tomas más medicina?. . . No me hágas casa, William."

Casbah house in the smell of dust and we made it. . . empty eukodal boxes stacked four feet along the walls. . .dead on the surplus blankets. . .girl screaming . . . *vecinos* rush in. . .

"What did she die of?"

"I don't know she just died."

Bill Gains in Mexico City room with his douche bag and his stash of codeine pills powdered in a bicarbonate can. "I'll just say I suffer from indigestion." coffee and blood spilled all over the place. cigarette holes in the pink blanket. . . The Consul would give me no information other than place of burial in The American Cemetery.

"Broke? Have you no pride? Go to your Consul." He gave me an alarm clock ran for a year after his death.

Leif repatriated by the Danish. freight boat out of Casa for Copenhagen sank off England with all hands. Remember my medium of distant fingers?—

"What did she die of?"

"End."

"Some things I find myself."

The Sailor went wrong in the end. hanged to a cell door by his principals: "Some things I find myself doing I'll pack in is all."

Bread knife in the heart. . .rub and die. . .repatriated by a morphine script. . .those out of Casa for Copenhagen on special yellow note. . .

"All hands broke? Have you no pride?" Alarm clock ran for a year. "He just sit down on the curb and die." Esperanza told me on Niño Perdido and we cashed a morphine script. those Mexican Nar. scripts on special yellow bank-note paper. . .like a thousand dollar bill . . .or a Dishonorable Discharge from the US Army. . . And fixed in the cubicle room you reach by climbing this ladder.

Yesterday call flutes of Ramadan: "*No me hágas casa.*"

Blood spill over shirts and light. the American trailing in form. . . He went to Madrid. This frantic Cuban fruit finds Kiki with a *novia* and stabs him with a kitchen knife in the heart. (Girl screaming. Enter the nabors.)

"Quédase con su medicina, William."

Half bottle of Fundador after half cure in the Jew Hospital. shots of demerol by candlelight. They turned off the lights and water. Paper-like dust we made it. Empty walls. Look anywhere. No good. *No bueno.*

He went to Madrid. . . Alarm clock ran for yesterday. . . *"No me hágas casa."* Dead on arrival. . . you might say at the Jew Hospital. . . blood spilled over the American. . . trailing lights and water. . . The Sailor went so wrong somewhere in that grey flesh. . . He just sit down on zero. . . I nodded on Niño Perdido his coffee over three hours late. . . They all went away and sent papers. . . The Dead Man write for you like a major. . . Enter *vecinos.* . . Freight boat smell of rectal mucus went down off England with all dawn smell of distant fingers. . . About this time I went to your Consul. He gave me a Mexican after his death. . . Five times of dust we made it. . . with soap bubbles of withdrawal crossed by a thousand junky nights. . . Soon after the half maps came in by candlelight. . . OCCUPY. . . Junk lines falling. . . Stay off. . . Bill Gains in the Yellow Sickness. . . Looking at dirty pictures casual as a ceiling fan short-timing the dawn we made it in the corn smell of rectal mucus and carbolic soap. . . familiar face maybe from the vacant lot. . . trailing tubes and wires. . . "You fucking-can't-wait-hungry-junkies! . . ." Burial in the American Cemetery. *"Quédase con su medicina. . ."* On Niño Perdido the girl screaming. . . They all went way through Casbah House. . . "Couldn't you write me any better than that? Gone away. . . You can look any place."

No good. *No Bueno.*

You wouldn't believe how hot things were when I left the States—I knew this one pusher wouldn't carry any shit on his person just shoot it in the line—Ten twenty grains over and above his own absorption according to the route he was servicing and piss it out in bottles for his customers so if the heat came up on them they cop out as degenerates—So Doc Benway assessed the situation and came up with this brain child—

"Once in the Upper Baboonasshole I was stung by a scorpion—the sensation is not dissimilar to a fix—Hummm."

So he imports this special breed of scorpions and feeds them on metal meal and the scorpions turned a phosphorescent blue color and sort of hummed. "Now we must find a worthy vessel," he said—So we flush out this old goof ball artist and put the scorpion to him and he turned sort of blue and you could see he was fixed right to metal—These scorpions could travel on a radar beam and service the clients after Doc copped for the bread—It was a good thing while it lasted and the heat couldn't touch us—However all these scorpion junkies began to glow in the dark and if they didn't score on the hour metamorphosed into scorpions straight away—So there was a spot of bother and we had to move on disguised as young junkies on the way to Lexington—Bill and Johnny we sorted out the names but they keep changing like one day I would wake up as Bill the next day as Johnny—So there we are in the train compartment shivering junk sick our eyes watering and burning.

Who Am I to Be Critical?

AND ALL OF A SUDDEN the sex chucks hit me in the crotch and I sagged against the wall and looked at Johnny too weak to say anything, it wasn't necessary, he was there too and without a word he dipped some soap in warm water and dropped my shorts and rubbed the soap on my ass and worked his cock up me with a corkscrew motion and we both came right away standing there and swaying with the train clickety clack clack spurt spurt into the brass cuspidor—We never got to Lexington actually—Stopped off in the town of Marshal and hit this old country croaker for tincture with the aged mother suffering from piles in the worst form there is line and he wrote like a major—That night we got into a pool game and Doc won a Dusenberg Panama hat tan suit and dark glasses like 1920 sports and the further South we went the easier it was to score like we brought the twenties along with us—Well we come to this Mexican border town in time to see something interesting—In order to make way for a new bridge that never got built actually they had torn down a block of shacks along the river where the Chink railway workers used to smoke the black stuff and the rats had been down under the shacks hooked for generations—So the rats was running all through the street squealing sick biting everyone in sight—When we went to look for our car couldn't find it and no cars anywhere just this train left over from an old Western—The track gave out somewhere north of Monterrey and we bought some horses off a Chinaman for a tin of mud—By this time there were soldiers everywhere shooting the civilians so we scored for some Civil War uniforms and joined one of the warring powers—And captured five soldiers who were wearing uniforms of a different color and the General got drunk and decided to hang the prisoners just for jolly and we rigged up a cart with a drop under a tree limb—The first one dropped straight and clean and one of the soldiers wiped his mouth and stepped forward grinning and pulled his pants down to an ankle and his cock flipped out spurting—We all stood there watching and feeling it right down to our toes and the others who were waiting to be hanged felt it too—So we stripped them and they got hard-ons waiting—They couldn't help it you understand. That night we requisitioned a ranch house and all got drunk and Johnny did this dance with his tie around his neck lolling his head on one side and letting his tongue fall out and wriggled his ass and dropped his pants and his cock flipped out and the soldiers rolled around laughing till they pissed all over themselves—Then they rigged up a harness under his arms and hoisted him up off the floor to a beam and gang-fucked him—By the time we got to Monterrey there was Spaniards around in armor like a costume movie and again we were lucky to arrive just at the right time. There was a crowd of people in the Zoco and we pushed up front with our rush-hour technique and saw they were getting ready to burn some character at the stake—When they lit the faggots at his feet the only sound you could hear was the fire crackling and then everyone sucked in his breath together and the screams tore through me and my lips and tongue swole up with blood and I come in my pants—And I could see others had shot their load too and you could smell it like a compost heap, some of us so close our pants steamed in the fire just pulling the screams and the smoke down into our lungs and sort of whimpering—It was tasty I tell you—So we hit Mexico City just before sunrise and I said here we go again—That heart pulsing in the sun and my cock pulsed right with it and jissom seeped through my thin cotton trousers and fell in the dust and shit of the street—And a boy next to me grinning and gave me a backhand pickpocket feel, my cock still hard and aching like after a wet dream—And we crawled up onto a muddy shelf by the canal and made it there three times slow fuck on knees in the stink of sewage looking at the black water—It turned out later this kid had the epilepsy—When he got these fits he would flop around and come maybe five times in his dry goods, made you feel good all over to watch it—He really had it built in and he told me he could fix it with a magic man we trade places—So we started off on foot across the mountains and down the other side to high jungle warm and steamy and he kept having these fits and I dug it special fucking him in the spasm his asshole fluttering like a vibrator—Well we come to this village and found the magic man in a little hut on the outskirts—An evil old character with sugary eyes that stuck to you—We told him what we wanted and he nodded and looked at both of us and smiled and said he would have to cook up the medicine we should come back next day at sundown—So we came back and he gave us the bitter medicine in clay pots—And I hadn't put the pot down before the pictures started coming in sharp and clear: the hanged boy pulling his legs up to the chin and pumping out the spurts by the irrigation ditch, the soldiers swinging me around in the harness, the burned man screaming away like a good one and that heart just pulsing and throwing off spurts of blood in the rising sun—Xolotl was explaining to me that only one body is left in the switch they were going to hang me and when I shot my load and died I would pass into his body—I was paralyzed by the medicine any case and they stripped me and lashed my body with special type sex nettles that burned and stung all over and my tongue swole up and gagged me and my eyes blurred over with blood—They rigged up a gallows with a split-bamboo platform and a ladder and I start up the ladder Xolotl goosing me and stood under the noose and he tightens it around my neck muttering spells and then gets down on the floor leaving me alone up there on the platform with the noose waiting—I saw him reach up with an obsidian knife and cut the rope held the platform and I fell and silver light popped in my eyes like a flash bulb—I got a whiff of ozone and penny arcades and then I felt it start way down in my toes these bone wrenching spasms emptied me and everything spilled out shit running down the back of my thighs and no control in my body paralyzed, twisting up in these spasms the jissom just siphoned me right into Xolotl's cock and next thing I was in his ass and balls flopping around spurting all over the floor and that evil old fuck crooning and running his hands over me so nasty—But then who am I to be critical?—I stayed there in the magic man's hut for three days sleeping and woke up the lookout different—And the magic man gave me some medicine to control the fits and I headed on south—Came at sundown to a clear river where boys were swimming naked—And one of them turned grinning with a hard-on and shoved his finger in and out his fist and I fell in one of my fits so they all had a go at me—The cold mountain shadows came down and touched my naked ass and I went back with the boy to his hut and ate beans and chili and lay with him on the floor breathing the pepper smell of his belches and stayed there with him and worked his patch of corn on the side of the mountain—That boy could keep a hard-on all night and I used to stick peppers up my ass when he fucked me like my guts was on fire—Well maybe I would be there still, work all day and after the work knocked out no words no thoughts just sit there looking at the blue mountains and ate and belched and fucked and slept same thing day after day the greatest—But one day we scored for a bottle of mescal and got lushed and he looked at me and said: "*Chinga de puto* I will rid the earth of you in the name of Jesus Christu!" and charges me with a machete—Well I'd seen it coming and tossed a cup of mescal in his eyes and side-stepped and he fell on his face and I rammed the planting stick right into the base of his brain—So that was that—And started South again and came finally to this spot where a lot of citizens were planting corn with sticks all working in concert, I didn't like the look of it but I was strung out for groceries and decided to make contact a mistake as it turned out—Because as soon as I walked out into that field I felt this terrible weight on me and there I was planting corn with them and everything I did and thought was already done and thought and there was this round of festivals where the priests put on lobster suits and danced around snapping their claws like castanets and nothing but maize maize maize—And I guess I would be there yet fructifying the maize God except for this one cat who was in Maya drag like me but I could see he was a foreigner too—He was very technical and a lovely fellow—He began drawing formulas on the floor and showed me how the priests operated their control racket: "It's like with the festivals and the fucking corn they know what everybody will see and hear and smell and taste and that's what thought is and these thought units are represented by symbols in their books and they rotate the symbols around and around on the calender." And as I looked at his formulas something began to crack up in my brain and I was free of the control beam and next thing we both got busted and sentenced to "Death in Centipede" —So they strapped us to couches in a room under the temple and there was a terrible smell in the place full of old bones and a centipede about ten feet long comes nuzzling out of one corner—So I turn on something I inherit from Uranus where my grandfather invented the adding machine—I just lay there without any thought in tons focus of heavy blue silence and a slow wave went through me and spread out of me and the couch began shaking and the tremors spread into the ground and the roof fell in and crushed the centipede and smashed the couch so the straps were loose and I slipped out and untied Technical Tilly—So we got out of there dodging stellae and limestone skulls as the whole temple came down in chunks and the wind blowing a hurricane brought in a tidal wave and there wasn't much left of the whole set when things cleared away—All the workers were running around loose now looking for the priests—The head priest was paralyzed and had turned into a centipede—We found him in a cubby hole under the rubble along with some others who were half crab or in various stages of disgusting metamorphosis—And

I figured we should do something special with these characters they are wise guys—So we organize this "fun fest" and made some obsidian jockstraps strung together with copper wire and heated the straps up white-hot and slipped them on, the priests did a belly dance like you used to see it in burlesque and we sat there yelling: "Take it off Take it off," laughing till we pissed and shit and came—You never heard such laughing with the control gone and goosing them with hot copper pricks—And others we put weights on their backs and dragged them through wooden troughs with flint flakes sticking up and so on—Fun and games what? Well after that none of us could look at corn and the grocery problem became acute—So we organize this protection racket shaking down the agriculturals—"It could happen again here—Kick in or else"—And they kicked in come level on average—Well groceries—And I had perfected a gimmick to keep my boys in line—I was still subject to these fits but I had learned to control the images—That is just before I flipped out I could put any image in the projector and—Action—Camera—Take—It always happened the way I took it and any character gave me any static was taken care of that way—But the boys from the North were moving in whole armies so we packed in and shifted to the hunting and fishing lark—I picked thirty of the most likely and suitable lads all things considered and we moved South up over the mountains and down the other side into jungle then up and over again getting monotonous—Piecing out the odds best we could spot of this and a spot of that—Once in a while I had to put it about with the earthquakes but come level on average what you might call a journeyman thief—Well fever and snakes and rapids and boys dropping out here and there to settle down with the locals I had no mob left when I run up against this really evil setup—The Chimu were something else—So we hit this town and right away I don't like it.

"Something here, John—Something wrong—I can feel it."

To begin with the average Chimu is unappetizing to say the least—Lips eaten off by purple and orange skin conditions like a baboon's ass and pus seeping out a hole where the nose should be disgust you to see it—And some of them are consisting entirely of penis flesh and subject to blast jissom right out their skull and fold up like an old wine bag—Periodically the Chimu organize fun fests where they choose up sides and beat each other's brains out with clubs and the winning team gang-fucks the losers and cut their balls off right after to make pouches for coco leaves they are chewing all the time green spit dripping off them like a cow with the aftosa—All things considered I was not innarrested to contact their loutish way of life—In the middle of this town was a construction of clay cubicles several stories high and I could see some kinda awful crabs were stirring around inside it but couldn't get close because the area around the cubicle is covered with black bones and hot as a blasting furnace—They had this heat weapon you got it?—Like white-hot ants all over you—Meanwhile I had been approached by the Green Boys have a whole whore house section built on catwalks over the mud flats entirely given over to hanging and all kinds death in orgasm young boys need it special—They were beautiful critters and swarmed all over me night and day smelling like a compost heap —But I wasn't buying it sight unseen and when I proposed to watch a hanging they come on all indignant like insulted whores—So I am rigged up a long distance periscope with obsidian mirrors Technical Tillie moaning about the equipment the way he always does and we watched them hang this boy just down from the country—Well I saw that when his neck snapped and he shot his load instead of flowing into the Green Boy the way nature intended these hot crabs hatched out of his spine and scoffed the lot.

So we organize the jungle tribes and take Boy's Town and confine the Green Boys in a dormitory, they are all in there turning cartwheels and giggling and masturbating and playing flutes—That was our first move to cut the supply line—Then after we had put the squeeze on and you could hear them scratching around in the cubicle really thin now we decided to attack—I had this special Green Boy I was making it with who knew the ropes you might say and he told me we have to tune the heat wave out with music—So we get all the Indians and all the Green Boys with drums and flutes and copper plates and stayed just out of the heat blast beating the drums and slowly closed in—Iam had rigged up a catapult to throw limestone boulders and shattered the cubicle so we move in with spears and clubs and finish them off and smashed the heat-sending set that was a living radio with insect parts—We turn the Green Boys loose and on our way rejoicing—

So down into the jungle on the head-shrinking lark—Know how it operates—You got these spells see? confines the citizen to his head under your control like you can shrink up all the hate in the area—What a gimmick but as usual I got greedy and the wind up is I don't have a head left to stand on—Sure I had the area sewed up but there wasn't any area left—Always was one to run things into the ground—Well there I was on the bottom when I hear about this virgin tribe called the Camuyas embrace every stranger and go naked all the time like nature intended and I said "the Camuyas are live ones" and got down there past all these bureaucrats with The Internal Indian Service doubted the purity of my intentions—But I confounded them with my knowledge of Mayan archaeology and the secret meaning of the centipede motif and Iam was very technical so we established ourselves as scientists and got the safe conduct—Those Camuyas were something else all naked rubbing up against you like dogs—They were sweet little critters and I might be there still except for a spot of bother with The Indian Commission about this hanging ceremony I organize figuring to trade in the chassis and renew my substance —So they chucked me out and talked usefully about that was that—And I made it up to the Auca who were warlike and wangled two healthy youths for a secret weapon—So took these boys out into the jungle and laid it on the line and one of them was ready to play ball and —spare you the monotonous details—Suffice it to say the Upper Amazon gained a hustler and there I was caught in the middle of all these feuds—Some one knocks off your cousin twice removed and you are obligated to take care of his great uncle—Been through all this before—Every citizen you knock off there are ten out looking for you geometric and I don't want to know—So I got a job with the Total Oil Company and that was another mistake—

Rats was running all over the morning—Somewhere North of Monterrey went into the cocaine business—By this time fish tail Cadillac—people—civilians—So we score for some business and get rich over the warring powers—shady or legitimate the same fuck of a different color and the general on about the treasure—We rigged their stupid tree limb and drop the alien corn—spot of business to Walgreen's—So we organize this 8267 kicked in level on average ape—Melodious gimmick to keep the boys in line—I had learned to control Law 334 procuring an orgasm by any image, Mary sucking him and running the outfield—Static was taken care of that way—what you might call a vending machine and boys dropping to Walgreen's—We are not locals. We sniff the losers and cut their balls off chewing all kinds masturbation and self-abuse like a cow with the aftosa—Young junkies return it to the white reader and one day I would wake up as Bill covered with ice and burning crotch—drop my shorts and comes gibbering up me with a corkscrew motion—We both come right away standing and trying to say something—I see other marks are coming on with the mother tincture—The dogs of Harry J. Anslinger sprouted all over me—By now we had word dust stirring the 1920's, maze of dirty pictures and the house hooked for generations—We all fucked the boy burglar feeling it right down to our toes—Spanish cock flipped out spurting old Montgomery Ward catalogues—So we stripped a young Dane and rigged the Yankee dollar—Pants down to the ankle, a barefoot Indian stood there watching and feeling his friend—Others had shot their load too over a broken chair through the tool heap—Tasty spurts of jissom across the dusty floor—Sunrise and I said here we go again with the knife—My cock pulsed right with it and trousers fell in the dust and dead leaves—Return it to the white reader in stink of sewage looking at open shirt flapping and comes maybe five times his ass fluttering like—We sniff what we wanted pumping out the spurts open shirt flapping—What used to be me in my eyes like a flash bulb, spilled adolescent jissom in the bath cubicle—Next thing I was Danny Deever in Maya drag—That night we requisitioned a Peruvian boy—I would pass into his body—What an awful place it is—most advanced stage—foreigner too—They rotate the symbols around IBM machine with cocaine—fun and games what?

Public Agent

So I am a public agent and don't know who I work for, get my instructions from street signs, newspapers and pieces of conversation I snap out of the air the way a vulture will tear entrails from other mouths. In any case I can never catch up on my back cases and currently assigned to intercept blue movies of James Dean before the stuff gets to those queers supporting a James Dean habit which, so long as this agent picks his way through barber shops, subway toilets, grope movies and Turkish Baths, will never be legal and exempt narcotic.

The first one of the day I nailed in a subway pissoir: "You fucking nance!" I screamed. "I'll teach you to savage my bloody meat, I will." And I sloughed him with the iron glove and his face smashed like rotten cantaloupe. Then I hit him in the lungs and blood jumped out his mouth, nose and eyes, spattered three commuters across the room huddled in gabardine topcoats and grey flannel suits under that. The broken fruit was lying with his head damning the piss running over his face and the whole trough a light pink from his blood. I winked at the commuters. "I can smell them fucking queers," I sniffed warningly. "And if there's one thing lower than a nance it's a spot of bloody grass. Now you blokes wouldn't be the type turn around and congor a pal's balls off would you now?" They arranged themselves on the floor like the three monkeys: See No Evil, Hear No Evil, and Speak No Evil.

"I can see you're three of our own," I said warmly and walked into the corridor where schoolboys chase each other with machetes, joyous boy-cries and zipper guns echo through the mosaic caverns. I pushed into a Turkish Bath and surprised a faggot brandishing a deformed erection in the steam room and strangled him straightaway with a soapy towel. I had to check in. I was thin now, barely strength in my receding flesh to finish off that tired faggot. I got into my clothes shivering and gaping and walked into the terminal drugstore. Five minutes to twelve. Five minutes to score. I walked over to the night clerk and threw a piece of tin on him.

Piss running over his face. Don't know who I work for. I get mine from his blood, newspapers and pieces. "I can smell them fucking the air the way a vulture will." In any case bloody grass. I sloughed him with the iron room and strangled him like rotten cantaloupe.

Then I had to check in. I was the blood jumped out his mouth, nose receding flesh to finish. Across the room huddled my clothes shivering grey flannel suits under terminal drugstore. So I am a public agent and the whole trough a light pink instruction from street. I winked at the commuters. "Conversation I snap out of queers," I sniffed warningly. "It's a spot up on my back cases." Queers supporting the floor like the three monkeys. "Grope movies and Turkish our own," I said warmly and walked exempt narcotic. Cool boys chase each other with the first one of the day. To a Turkish Bath and surprised you bloody nance. Soapy towel glove hit him in the lungs and eyes spattered: Ping! And walked into the gabardine topcoats. Five minutes to that broken fruit.

"Treasury Department," I said. "Like to check your narcotic inventory against RX. . . How much you using young fellow?" Shaking my head and pushing all the junk bottles and scripts into my brief case: "I hate to see a young man snafu his life script. . . Maybe I can do something for you. That is if you promise me to take the cure and stay off."

"I promise anything. I gotta wife and kids."

"Just don't let me down is all."

I walked out and got straight in the lu of the Bus Terminal Chinese Restaurant. It's a quiet place with very bad food. But what a John for a junky.

Well I checked into the old Half-Moon Hotel you can get to the lobby through the subway and walked in on the wrong room, an ether party, with my cigarette lit and everyone's lung blew out about six characters, cats and chicks. So I get a face full of tits and spare ribs and throat gristle. . . All in the day's work. . . Follow up on it. Score. I walked the gabardine top tin on him. The broken fruit. Piss running over his face. "Like to check your narcotic inventor. I get mine from his blood."

"Much you using young fellow?"

"I can smell them fucking all the junk bottles and scripts." In any case bloody grass. . . See a young man snafu his and strangled him like rot do something for you in the blood. Jumped cure and stay off to finish. Grey flannel suits under all public agents of the bus from street. Grope movie and walked in on the wrong room warmly. Exempt light and lungs. And eyes spattered night clerk and threw a piece of coats. "Five minutes to Treasury Department," I said. Shaking my head and pushing the air the way a vulture will into my brief case. I hate sloughed him with the iron room life script. Maybe I can cantaloupe. Them I had to check you. Promise me to take out his mouth, nose receding flesh.

"I promise anything. I go huddled my clothes shivering." I walked out and got light pink instructions terminal Chinese commuters. Hit him in the lungs the day's work. Follow up. A word about my work. The Human Issue has been called in by the Home Office. Engineering flaws you know. There is the work of getting it off the shelves and that is what I do. We are not interested in the individual models, but in the mold, the human die. This must be broken. You never see any live ones up here in Freelandt. Too many patrols. It's a dull territory unless you enjoy shooting a paralyzed swan in a cesspool. Of course there are always the Outsiders. And the young ones I dig special. Long Pigs I call them. Give myself a treat and do it slow just feeding on the subject's hate and fear and the white stuff oozes out when they crack sweet as a lobster claw. . . I hate to put out the eyes because they are my water hole. They call me the Meat Handler. Among other things.

I had business with the Egyptian. My time was running out. He was sitting in a mosaic café with stone shelves along the walls and jars of colored syrups sipping a heavy green drink.

"I need the time milking," I said.

He looked at me, his eyes eating erogenous holes. His face got an erection and turned purple. And we went into the vacant lot behind the café naked to a turn.

White men killed at a distance. Don't know the answer, do you?

Den Mark of Trak in every face: "Death, take over."

"Never nobody liked dancing no better than Red."

"Let's dance," he said.

The script for shit, "Here you are, sir," and I could see he was heavy with the load. Outfields and back to Moscow for liquidation. I had business with the Gyp. Trak in every kidney. The script for heavy drink. His eyes got an erection and turned the effluvia and became addicts of vacant lot. My time was running out its last black grains.

Trak Trak Trak

THE SAILOR AND I burned down The Republic of Panama from Darien swamps to David trout streams on paregoric and goof balls—(Note: Nembutal)—You lose time putting a con down on a Tiddlywink chemist—"No glot—Clom Fliday"—(Footnote: old time junkies will remember—Used to be a lot of Chinese pushers in the 1920's but they found the West so unreliable dishonest and wrong when an Occidental junky comes to score they say: "No glot—Clom Fliday.")

And we were running short of substitute buyers—They fade in silver mirrors of 1910 under a ceiling fan—Or we lost one at dawn in a wisp of rotten sea wind—Out in the bay little red poison sea snakes swim desperately in sewage—Camphor sweet cooking paregoric smells billow from the mosquito nets—The termite floor gave under our feet spongy and rotten—The albatross at dawn on rusty iron roofs—

"Time to go, Bill," said the Sailor, morning light on cold coffee.

"I'm thin"—Crisscross of broken light from wood lathes over the patio, silver flak holes in his face—We worked the Hole together in our lush rolling youth—(Footnote: "working the Hole," robbing drunks on the subway)—And kicked a habit in East St. Louis—Made it four times third night, fingers scraping bone—At dawn shrinking from flesh and cloth—

Hands empty of hunger on the stale breakfast table—winds of sickness through his face—pain of the long slot burning flesh film—canceled eyes, old photo fading—violet brown souvenir of Panama City—I flew to La Paz trailing the colorless death smell of his sickness with me still, thin air like death in my throat—sharp winds of black dust and the grey felt hat on every head—purple pink and orange disease faces cut pre-natal flesh, genitals under the cracked bleeding feet—aching lungs in dust and pain wind—mountain lakes blue and cold as liquid air—Indians shitting along the mud walls—brown flesh, red blankets—

"No, señor. Necesita receta."

And the refugee German croaker you hit anywhere: "This you must take orally—You will inject it of course—Remember it is better to suffer a month if so you come out—With this habit you lose the life is it not?" And he gives me a long creepy human look—

And Joselito moved into my room suffocating me with soccer scores—He wore my clothes and we laid the same *novia* who was thin and sickly always making magic with candles and Virgin pictures and drinking aromatic medicine from a red plastic eye cup and never touched my penis during the sex act.

Through customs checks and control posts and over the mountains in a blue blast of safe conducts and three monkey creatures ran across the road in a warm wind—(sound of barking dogs and running water) swinging round curves over the misty void—down to end of the road towns on the edge of Yage country where shy Indian cops checked our papers—through broken stellae, pottery fragments, worked stones, condoms and shit-stained comics, slag heaps of phosphorescent metal excrement—faces eaten by the pink and purple insect disease of the New World—crab boys with human legs and genitals crawl out of clay cubicles—Terminal junkies hawk out crystal throat gristle in the cold mountain wind—Goof ball bums covered with shit sleep in rusty bathtubs—a delta of sewage to the sky under terminal stasis, speared a sick dolphin that surfaced in bubbles of coal gas—taste of metal left silver sores on our lips—only food for this village built on iron racks over an iridescent lagoon—swamp delta to the sky lit by orange gas flares.

In the flash bulb of orgasm I saw three silver numbers —We walked into the streets and won a football pool —Panama clung to our bodies stranger color through his eyes the lookout different.

Flash bulb monster crawling inexorably from Old Fred Flash—the orgasm in a 1920 movie, silver writing from backward countries—Flapping genitals in wind—explosion of the throat from peeled noon drifting sheets of male flesh to a stalemate of black lagoons while open shirts twist iridescent in the dawn—(this sharp smell of carrion.)

"Take it from a broken stalemate—The Doctor couldn't reach and see?: Those pictures are the line—Fading breath on bed showed sound track—You win handful of dust that's what."

Metamorphosis of the Rewrite Department coughing and spitting in fractured air—flapping genitals of carrion—Our drained countess passed on a hideous leather body—We are digested and become nothing here—dust air of gymnasiums in another country and besides old the pool now, a few inches on dead post cards—here at the same time there his eyes—Silver light popped stroke of nine.

Dead post card you got it?—Take it from noon refuse like ash—Hurry up see?—Those pictures *are* yourself—Is backward sound track—That's what walks beside you to a stalemate of physical riders—("You come with me, Meester?")—I knew Mexican he carried in his flesh with sex acts shooting them pills I took—Total alertness she is your card—Look, simple: Place exploded man goal in other flesh—dual controls country—double sex sad as the Drenched Lands.

Last man with such explosion of the throat crawling inexorably from something he carried in his flesh—Last turnstile was in another country and besides knife exploded Sammy the Butcher—Holes in 1920 movie—Newspaper tape fading, after dinner sleep ebbing carbon dioxide—Indications enough showed you calls to make, horrors crawling inexorably toward goal in other flesh—What are you waiting for, kid?—Slotless human wares?—Nothing here now—Metamorphosis is complete—Rings of Saturn in the dawn—The sky exploded question from vacant lots—youth nor age but as it were lips fading—There in our last film mountain street boy exploded "the word," sits quietly silence to answer.

"You come with me, Meester to greet the garbage man and the dawn? Traced fossil countenance everlastingly about the back door, Meester." sick dawn of inane cooperation—dead post cards swept out by typewriters clatter hints as we shifted commissions—Hurry up please—Crawling inexorably toward its goal—I—We—They—sit quietly in last terrace of the garden—The neon sun sinks in this sharp smell of carrion—(circling albatross—peeled noon—refuse like ash)—Ghost of Panama clung to our throats coughing and spitting in the fractured air, falling through space between worlds, we twisted slowly to black lagoons, flower floats and gondolas—tentative crystal city iridescent in the dawn wind—(adolescents ejaculate over the tide flats)—Dead post card are you thinking of?—What thinking?—peeled noon and refuse like ash—Hurry up please—Make yourself a bit smart—Who is the third that walks beside you to a stalemate of black lagoons and violet light? Last man—Phosphorescent centipede feeding on flesh strung together we are digested and become nothing here.

"You come with me, Meester?"

Up a great tidal river to the port city stuck in water hyacinths and banana rafts—The city is an intricate split-bamboo structure in some places six stories high overhanging the street propped up by beams and sections of railroad track and concrete pillars, an arcade from the warm rain that falls at half hour intervals—The coast people drift in the warm steamy night eating colored ices under the arc lights and converse in slow catatonic gestures punctuated by immobile silence—Plaintive boy-cries drift through Night Of the Vagrant Ball Players.

"Paco!—Joselito!—Enrique!—"

"*A ver Luckees!*"

"Where you go, Meester?"

"Squeezed down heads?"

Soiled mouth above a tuxedo blows smoke rings into the night, "SMOKE TRAK CIGARETTES. THEY LIKE YOU. TRAK LIKE ANY YOU. ANY TRAK LIKE YOU. SMOKE TRAKS. THEY SERVICE. TRAK TRAK TRAK."

Los Vagos Jugadores de Pelota storm the stale streets of commerce—Civil Guards discreetly turn away and open their flys to look for crabs in a vacant lot—For the Vagrant Ball Players can sound a Hey Rube Switch brings a million adolescents shattering the customs barriers and frontiers of time, swinging out of the jungle with Tarzan cries, crash landing perilous tin planes and rockets, leaping from trucks and banana rafts, charge through the black dust of mountain wind like death in the throat.

The trak sign stirs like a nocturnal beast and bursts into blue flame, "SMOKE TRAK CIGARETTES. THEY LIKE YOU. TRAK LIKE ANY YOU. ANY TRAK LIKE YOU. SMOKE TRAKS. THEY SATISFY. THEY SERVICE. TRAK TRAK TRAK."

"Vagos Jugadores de Pelota, *sola esperanza del mundo*, take it to Cut City—Street gangs Uranian born in the face of nova conditions, cut word lines, cut time lines—Take it to Cut City, *muchachos*—'Minutes to go'—"

Jungle invades the weed grown parks where armadillos infected with the Earth Eating Disease gambol through deserted kiosks and Bolivar in catatonic limestone liberates the area—Candiru infiltrate causeways and swimming pools—Albinos blink in the sun—rank smell of rotten rivers and mud flats—swamp delta to the sky that does not change—islands of garbage where Green Boys with delicate purple gills tend chemical gardens—terminal post card shrinking in heavy time. Muttering addicts of the orgasm drug, boneless in the sun, eaten alive by crab men—terminal post card shrinking in heavy time. "Thing Police keep all Board Room Reports—Do not forget this, *Señor*—"

They were searching his room when he returned from the Ministry of Tourist Travel—Fingers light and cold as Spring wind rustling papers and documents—One flashed a badge like a fish side in dark water—

"Police, Johnny."

"Campers," obviously—"Campers" move into any

government office and start issuing directives and spinning webs of inter-office memos—Some have connections in high sources that will make the operation legal and exempt narcotic—Others are shoestring operators out of broom closets and dark rooms of the Mugging Department—They charge out high on ammonia issuing insane orders and requisitioning any object in their path—Tenuous bureaus spring up like sandstorms—The whole rancid oil scandal drifted out in growth areas—

Bradly was reading the sign nailed to a split-bamboo tenement—The sign was printed on white paper book page size:

Cut The Sex and Dream Utility Lines//

Cut the Trak Service Lines//

The paws do not refresh//

Clom Fliday Meester Surplus Oil//

Working for the Yankee dollar?//

Trak your own utilities//

Under silent wings of malaria a tap on his shoulder: "*Documentes, señor. Passaport.*"

His passport drew them like sugar flashing gold teeth in little snarls of incredulity: "*Passaport no bueno. No en ordenes.*"

The fuzz that could not penetrate to the passport began chanting in unison: "*Comisaria! Comisaria!*

Comisaria! Meester a la Comisaria!—Passaport muy malo. No good. *No bueno.* Typical sights leak out." The Comandante wore a green uniform spattered with oil and gave out iron smoke as he moved—A small automatic moved round his waist on metal tracks trailing blue sparks—Seedy agents click into place with reports and documents.

"It is *permiso, si* to read the public signs. This"—his hand covered the white sign on a split-bamboo wall—"is a special case."

A man with a green eyeshade slid forward: "Yes. That's what they call it: 'making a case'—It's all there in the files, the whole rancid oil scandal of the Trak Sex And Dream Utilities in Growth Areas."

He pointed to a row of filing cabinets and lockers—Smell of moldy jockstraps and chlorine drifted through the police terminal. The Comandante turned the newspaper man back with a thin brown hand: "Much politics that one—It is better to be just technical."

A Swede con man hiding out in Rio Bamba under the cold souvenir of Chimborazi, junk cover removed for the nonpayment, syndicates of the world feeling for him with distant fingers of murder, perfected that art along the Tang Dynasty in the back room of a Chinese laundry. The Swede had one thing left: the grey felt hat concession for "growth areas" hidden under front companies and aliases. With a 1910 magic lantern he posed Indians in grey felt hats and broke the image into a million pieces reflected in dark eyes and blue mountain ice and black water and piss and lamp chimneys, tinted bureaucrat glasses, gun barrels, store fronts and café mirrors—He flickered the broken image into the eyes of a shrunken head that died in agony looking at a grey felt hat. And the Head radiated: HAT. .HAT. .HAT . .HAT. .HAT. .

"It is a jumping head," he said.

When the hat lines formed one thing that could break them was orgasm—So he captured a missionary's wife and flickered her with pornographic slides—And he took her head to radiate anti-sex—He took other anti-sex heads in coprophiliac vice and electric disgust—He dimed the Sex and Dream Utilities of the land. And he was shipped back to Sweden in a lead cylinder to found the Trak Service and the Trak Board.

Trak has come a long way from a magic lantern in the Chink laundry. The Heads were donated to the Gothenburg Museum where the comparatively innocuous emanations precipitated a mass sex orgy.

Vagos Jugadores, *sola esperanza del mundo,* take it to Cut City. the black obsidian pyramid of Trak Home Office.

"The perfect product, gentlemen, has precise molecular affinity for its client of predilection. Someone urges the manufacture and sale of products that wear out? This is not the way of competitive elimination. Our product never leaves the customer. We sell the Servicing and all Trak products have precise need of Trak servicing. . . The servicing of a competitor would act like antibiotic, offering to our noble Trak-strain services inedible counterpart. . . This is not just another habit-forming drug this is the habit-forming drug takes over all functions from the addict including his completely unnecessary under the uh circumstances and cumbersome skeleton. Reducing him ultimately to the helpless condition of a larva. He may be said then to owe his very life such as it is to Trak servicing. . ."

The Trak Reservation so-called includes almost all areas in and about the United Republics of Freelandt and, since the Trak Police process all matters occurring in Trak Reservation and no one knows what is and is not Reservation cases, civil and criminal are summarily removed from civilian courts with the single word TRAK to unknown sanctions. . . Report meetings of Trak personnel are synchronized with other events as to a low pressure area. . . Benway was reporting so-called actually included almost the report meetings of Trak persons. . . Sometimes the Reservation is other persons and events in Trak guards sub type. . .

"Outskirts of Mexico City—Can't quite make it with all the guards around—Are you at all competent to teach me the language? Come in please with the images—"

Smell death bed pictures—Cooperation inane—Carrion in the bank—Passport bad—Average on level tore canines—Understand fee: Corpses hang pants open in erogenous smells to Monterrey—Clear and loud ahead naked post cards and baby shoes—A man comes back to something he left in underwear peeled the boy warm in 1929—Thighs slapped the bed jumped ass up—"Johnny Screw"—Cup is split—wastings—Thermodynamics crawls home—game of empty hands—bed pictures post dead question—carrion smell sharp.

"Meester, jelly thing win you—Waiting for this?"

Streets of idiot pleasure—obsidian palaces of the fish city, bubbles twisting slow linen to the floor, traced fossils of orgasm.

"You win something like jelly fish, Meester."

His eyes calm and sad as little cats snapped the advantages: "And I told him I said I am giving notice—Hanged in your dirty movies for the last time—Three thousand years in show business and I never stand still for such a routine like this."

Street boys of the green with cruel idiot smiles and translucent amber flesh, aromatic jasmine excrement, pubic hairs that cut needles of pleasure—serving insect pleasures of the spine—alternate terminal flesh when the egg cracks.

"This bad place, Meester—This place of last fuck for Johnny."

Smile of idiot death spasms—slow vegetable decay filmed his amber flesh—always there when the egg cracks and the white juice spurts from ruptured spines—From his mouth floated coal gas and violets—The boy dropped his rusty black pants—delicate must of soiled linen—clothes stiff with oil on the red tile floor—naked and sullen his street boy senses darted around the room for scraps of advantage—

"You come with me Meester? Last flucky."

Stranger color through his eyes the lookout different, face transparent with all the sewers of death—Hard-ons spread nutty smells through the outhouse—soiled linen under the ceiling fan—spectral lust of shuttered rooms —He left a shirt on my bed.

"Jimmy Sheffields is still as good as he used to be."

"He was servicing customers shit, Meester—So Doctor Benway snapped the advantages—This special breed spitting notice: Egg cracks the transmitter—Rat spines gathering mushroom flesh—The boy dropped around your room for scraps—Got the rag on body from vegetable—Dropped his pants and his cock."

"Who are you—My boat—"

"Smells through the outhouse—A compost heap, Meester."

Sacred Sewers of Death—Boy dropped under the swamp cypress flopping around in soiled linen—(Started off on foot across the deserted fields—a little hut on the outskirts—The writer looked at both of us good as he used to be.) Idiot pictures started coming in—

"You win something like jelly with his knees up to the chin—sad little irrigation ditch—Parrot on shoulder prods that heart—Paralyzed, twisting in your movies for the last time—Out of me from the waist down—I never stand still for such lookout on street boys of the green—Happened that boy could keep his gas and violets—This spot advantages brown hands working in concert for a switch to the Drenched Lands—Cyclotron shit these characters—Come level on average smell under any image—Evil odors high around the other—Jimmy Sheffields is again as good—Street boy's breath receiving notice—Jelly routine like this—When the egg cracks our spines servicing special customers of fossil orgasm."

Kerosene lamp spattered light on red- and white-striped T-shirt and brown flesh—Dropped his pants—Pubic hairs cut stale underwear fan whiffs of young hard-on washing odors—afternoon wind where the awning flaps—

"Get physical with a routine like this?—Show you something interesting: diseased flesh servicing frantic last fuck for Johnny—Film over the bed you know, eyes pop out—Naked candy around the room, scraps of adolescent image, hot semen in Panama—Then the boy drops his drag and retires to a locker—*Who* lookout different? Who are *you* when their eyes pop out—Mandrake smells through the outhouse—The boy dropped and the boy wakes up paralyzed—Remember there is only one visit: iron roof—soiled linen under the clothes—scar tissue—shuttered room—evil odors of food—I wasn't all that far from being good as I used to be—Obsidian that broker before they get to him—A crab scuttles out heavy—You win something like vacant lot—sad little patch right?—boy face, green scarf—movies three up—You understand until I die work I never stand still for. and such got the job—End getting to know street boys of the Green Passport vending last fuck as his pants drop."

Dust of cities and wind faces came to World's End—call through remote dawn soaked in clouds, shivering back to mucus of the world.

Dust jissom in the bandanna trailing afternoon wind —under black Stetson peeled his stale underwear— Kerosene lamp spattered light on .22, delicate legs and brown flesh—clothes stiff in the locker room rubbing each other—sullen as the other two watched—Stranger dropped his pants—Brown hands spurt it to the chest—

"Find time buyer—Start job—Image under the same position—Change place of your defense—"

"A Johannesburg bidonville he was servicing—Customers shitting Nigger for an eyecup of degenerates— Ejaculated the next day as Johnny—Meal mouthed cunt suckers flow through you—This special breed spitting cotton travel on a radar beam of service proof shortbread—Shivering junk sick told your reporter the sex chucks hit us in heroin slow down—The paranoid ex-Communist was there—Rubbed Moscow up me with a corkscrew motion of his limestones—Split is the wastings of the pool game—irritably for Mexico—By now we had floppy city in the distance, 1920's faint and intermittent—The track gave out forever an inch from the false bottom—

"They had torn down the transmitter—Rats was running the post—Somewhere North of Monterrey we meet in warring powers—Captured the spine clinic and cook down the prisoners for jelly—We are accused of soliciting with prehensile tree limbs—The first one dropped your defense his mouth bleeding—Got the rag on— Waiting to see this exhibit, dropped his pants and I came the spectroscope—You could smell it like a compost heap, pants just pulling in the winds of Panhandle

—So we hit the Sacred Cotton Wood Grove—It's the only way to live—Jissom under the swamp cypress—and the warm Spring wind to feel my cock—(dead bird in the black swamp water)—He would flop around in the trees, come five times in his dry goods.

"He told me he could fix back places—a little hut on the outskirts—pale blue sugary eyes that stuck to you—The Writer looked at both of us and smiled a low pressure area, switch paper in his hands—weak and intermittent before the pictures started coming in: 'Lawd Lawd have you seen my boy with his knees up to the chin pumping out spurts by the irrigation ditch?'

"When I shot my load I was paralyzed from the medicine—Twisting in these spasms solid female siphoned out of me from the waist down—Shattering special type sex hangs from telegraph pole—And then I felt it way down in a carnival of splintered pink—

"Cold mountain shadows in the attic—And I went back with the boy to his cellar—Wonder whatever happened to that boy could keep a hard-on all night?—A man comes back to something looking at the blue mountains—Same thing day after day—World messages on the shit house wall—Cock spurting limestone—Summer dawn smell of boy balls so that was that—This spot where a lot of citizens will not work in concert—I didn't—Out for groceries and decided to whimper on the boys—We found Mother Green in your rubble along with some others from his deserted cock—Disgusting metamorphosis and a cyclotron shit these characters—

(You wouldn't have a rope would you?)—Maybe I'm asking too many agriculturals—

"Come level on average we'll hold that old cow in line—Put any image in the cold drink would you?—Wet back asleep with a hard-on was taken care of that way—Look, moving in whole armies and he sits me fishing lark—Silent and shaking things considered and we moved out hard—Around the other side piecing out the odds best we could—In the barn attic night and day smelling his thin cotton pants—He wakes buying it sight unseen.

"Jimmy busy doing *something* feller say—boys streaked with coal dust—Maybe I'm asking too many—(You wouldn't have a rope would you?)—Well now that bedroom sitter boy his cock came up wet sleep—Smiling looks at his crotch—Peeled slow and touch it—Springs out hard—Turns me around the end of his cock glistening—That smell through the dingy room clings to him like—Raw and peeled came to the hidden gallows—Open door underneath to cut down ghost assassins—Odor of semen drifts in the brain—Jimmy with cruel idiot smile shacks elbows twisting him over on his candy—Found a pajama cord and tied the boy—Jimmy lay there and suck his honey—Must have blacked out in the Mandrake Pub—So called Rock and Rollers crack wise on a lumpy studio bed with old shoes and overcoat some one cope—The boy wakes up paralyzed in hock—Sorted out name you never learned to use—Them marketable commodities turn you on direct connection come level on average—Whiff of dried jissom in the price—I was on the roof so sweet young breath came through the time buyer—

"The gate in white flames—Early answer to the boy wakes naked—Down on his stomach is he?—Ah there and iron cool in the mouth—Come see me tonight in bone wrenching spasms—Silver light pops something interesting—The boy features being younger of course —To your own people you frantic come level on average —Wait a bit—No good at this rate—Try one if you want worthless old shit screaming without a body—Roll two years operation completed—We are? Well the wind up is who?—*Quién es?*—World's End as a boy in drag retired to the locker—My page deals so many tasty ways on the bed—You know—Eyes pop out—Candy and cigarettes what? Rectum open, the warm muscle boy rampant and spitting adolescent image—Hot semen amuck in Panama—Scenic railways when their eyes pop out—Know the answer?—Two assholes and a mandrake—They'll do it every time—Rock and Rollers crack wise with overwhelming Minraud girl, wipe their ass on the women's toilet—And the boy wakes up paralyzed from arsenic and bleeding gums—Remember there is only one visit of a special kind—Flesh juice vampires is rotten smell of ice—No good *no bueno* outright or partially.

"Reason for the change of food he is subject to take back the keys—Square fact is that judges like it locked —Acting physician at Dankmoor fed up you understand until I die—End getting to know whose hanged man—One more chance still?—Come back to the Spanish bait, hard faced matron bandages the blotter—The shock when your neck breaks is far away—In this hotel room you are already dead of course—Boy stretches a leg, his cock flipped out—But uh well you see sputter of burning insect wings—"

In the sun at noon shirt open Kiki steps forward—With a wriggle stood naked spitting over the tide flats bare feet in dog's excrement—washed back on Spain repeat performance page.

Early Answer

PREDATED CHECKS BOUNCE all around us in green place by the ball park—Come and jack off—passport vending machines—Jimmy walked along North End Road—(Slow-motion horses pulling carts—boys streaked with coal dust)—a low-pressure area and the wind rising—Came to the World's End Pissoir and met a boy with wide shoulders, black eyes glinting under the street lights, a heavy silk scarf tucked into his red- and white-striped T-shirt—In the bedroom sitter the boy peeled off his clothes and sat down naked on the bed blowing cigarette smoke through his pubic hairs—His cock came up in the smoke—Switchblade eyes squinted, he watched with a smile wasn't exactly a smile as Jimmy folded his clothes—Raw and peeled, naked now his cock pulsing—Jimmy picked up his key and put it in his mouth sucking the metal taste—The other sat smoking and silent—A slow drop of lubricant squeezed out the end of his cock glistening in light from the street—Shutters clattered in the rising wind—A rotten vegetable smell seeped through the dingy room, shadow cars moved across the rose wall paper—

K9 had an appointment at The Sheffield Arms Pub but the short wave faded out on the location—Somewhere to the left? or was it to the right?—On? Off? North End Road?—He walked through empty market booths, shutters clattering—Wind tore the cover off faces he passed raw and peeled—Came to World's End wind blowing through empty time pockets—No Sheffield Arms—Back to his room full of shadows—There he was sitting on the bed with the smile that wasn't exactly a smile—At the washbasin a boy was using his toothbrush—

"Who are these people?"

The boy turned from the washbasin "You don't remember me?—Well we met in a way that is"—The toothbrush in his hand was streaked with blood.

Jimmy sat down on the bed his rectum tingling—The other picked up his scarf from a chair and ran it through his fingers looking at Jimmy with a cruel idiot smile—His hands closed on Jimmy's elbows twisting him over on his stomach down on the bed—The boy found a pajama cord and tied Jimmy's hands behind his back—Jimmy lay there gasping and sucked the key, tasting metal in his mouth—The other saddled Jimmy's Body—

He spit on his hands and rubbed the spit on his cock—He placed his hands on Jimmy's ass cheeks and shoved them apart and dropped a gob of spit on the rectum—He slid the scarf under Jimmy's hips and pulled his body up onto his cock—Jimmy gasped and moved with it—The boy slid the scarf up along Jimmy's body to the neck—

He must have blacked out though he hadn't had much to drink at the pub—two so-called double brandies and two Barley wines—He was lying on a lumpy studio bed in a strange room—familiar too—in shoes and overcoat—someone else's overcoat—such a coat he would never have owned himself—a tweedy loose-fitting powder-blue coat—K9 ran to tight-fitting black Chesterfields which he usually bought second-hand in hock shops—He had very little money for clothes though he liked to dress in "banker drag" he called it—black suits—expensive ties and linen shirts—Here he was in such a coat as he would never voluntarily have owned or worn—someone else's room—bed sitter—cheap furniture suitcases open—K9 found two keys covered with dust on the mantel—Sat down convenient and sorted out his name—

"You never learned to use your Jimmy—slow with the right—there will be others behind him with the scarf—We met you know in a way that is in the smell of wine—You don't remember me?"

Taste of blood in his throat familiar too—and overcoat—someone else's—streaked with coal dust—The bed sitter boy as it always does folded his clothes—Lay there gasping fresh in today—

"Went into what might be called the comfortable and got myself a flat jewelry lying about wholesale side—Learned how to value them marketable commodities come level on average—well groceries—She started screaming for a respectable price—I was on the roof so I had to belt her—Find a time buyer before doing sessions—There's no choice if they start job for instance—Have to let it go cheap and start further scream along the line—one or two reliable thieves—Work was steady at the gate to meet me—early answer to use on anyone considering to interfere—Once in a while I had to put it about but usually what you might call a journeyman thief—It was done so modern and convenient—Sorted out punishment and reward lark—On, off? the bed down on his stomach is he? Ah there you are behind him with the scarf—Hands from 1910—There's no choice if took off his clothes—Have to let it go cheap and start naked."

Twisted the scarf tighter and tighter around Jimmy's neck—Jimmy gasped coughing and spitting, face swollen with blood—His spine tingled—Coarse black hair suddenly sprouted all over him. Canines tore through his gum with exquisite toothache pain—He kicked in bone wrenching spasms. Silver light popped in his eyes.

He decided to take the coat with him—Might pass someone on the stairs and they would think he was the tenant since the boy resembled him in build and features being younger of course but then people are not observant come level on average—Careful—

"Careful—Watch the exits—wait a bit—no good at this rate—Watch the waves and long counts—no use moving out—try one if you want to—all dies in convulsions screaming without a body—Know the answer? —arsenic two years: operation completed—We are arsenic and bleeding gums—Who? *Quién es?*—World's End loud and clear—so conjured up wide shoulders and black eyes glinting—shadow cars through the dingy room—My page deals the bedroom sitter out of suitcase here on the bed where you know me with cruel idiot smile as Jimmy's eyes pop out—Silk scarf moved up rubbing—Pubic hair sprouted all over him tearing the flesh like wire—Eyes squinted from a smell I always feel—Hot spit burned his rectum open—The warm muscle contracts—Kicked breathless coughing and spitting adolescent image blurred in film smoke—through the gums the fist in his face—taste of blood—His broken body spurted life in other flesh—identical erections kerosene lamp—electric hair sprouted in ass and genitals—taste of blood in the throat—Hot semen spurted idiot mambo—one boy naked in Panama —Who?—*Quién es?*—Compost heap stench where you know me from—a smell I always feel when his eyes pop out—"

"Know the answer? arsenic two years: goof ball bum in 1910 Panama. They'll do it every time—Vampires is no good all possessed by overwhelming Minraud girl—"

"Are you sure they are not for protection?"

"Quite sure—nothing here but to borrow your body for a special purpose: ('Excellent—Proceed to the ice.') —in the blood arsenic and bleeding gums—They were addicted to this round of whatever visits of a special kind—An errand boy of such a taste took off his clothes —Indications enough naked now his cock healed scar tissue—Flesh juice vampires is no good—all sewage—sweet rotten smell of ice—no use of them better than they are—The whole thing tell you no good *no bueno* outright or partially."

"Reasons for the change of food not wholly disinterested—The square fact is that judges like a chair—For many years he used Parker—Fed up with present food in the Homicide Act and others got the job—So think before time that abolition is coming anyway after that, all the Top Jobbies would like to strike a bargain in return for accepting the end of hanging—Generous? Nothing—I wasn't all that far from ebbing in position—"

"Have to move fast—Nail that Broker before they get to him—Doing him a favor any case—"

He found the Broker in a café off the Socco—heavy with massive muscled flesh and cropped grey hair—K9 stood in the shadow and tugged his mind screen—The Broker stood up and walked down an alley—K9 stepped out of the shadows in his new overcoat—

"Oh it's you—Everything all right?—"

K9 took off his hat respectfully and covered his gun with it—He had stuffed the hat with the Green Boy's heavy silk scarf—a crude silencer but there was nobody in the alley—It wasn't healthy to be within earshot when the Broker had business with anyone—He stood with the hat an inch from the Broker's mid section—He looked into the cold grey eyes—

"Everything is just fine," he said—

And pumped three Police Specials into the massive stomach hard as a Japanese wrestler—The Broker's mouth flew open sucking for breath that did not come—K9 gave him three more and stepped aside—The Broker folded, slid along a wall and flopped face up his eyes glazing over—Lee dropped the burning hat and scarf on a pile of excrement and walked out of the alley powder smoke drifting from his cheap European suit—He walked toward flesh of Spain and Piccadilly—

"Wind hand to the hilt—Fed up you understand until I die—Work we have to do and way got the job—End getting to know whose reports are now ended—'One more change,' he said, 'touching circumstance'—Have you still—Come back to the Spanish bait it's curtains under his blotter."

Who? *Quién es?*—Question is far away—In this hotel room you are writing whiffs of Spain—Boy stretches a leg—His cock flipped out in the kerosene lamp—sputter of burning insect wings—Heard the sea—tin shack over the mud flats—erogenous holes and pepper smells—

In the sun at noon shirt open as his pants dropped—lay on his stomach and produced a piece of soap—rubbed the soap in—He gasped and moved with it

—whiffs of his feet in the warm summer afternoon—

Who? *Quién es?* It can only be the end of the world ahead loud and clear—

Kiki steps forward on faded photo—pants slipping down legs with a wriggle stood naked spitting on his hands—Shot a bucket grinning—over the whispering tide flats youths in the act, pants down, bare feet in dog's excrement—Street smells of the world siphoned back red-and-white T-shirt to brown Johnny—that stale dawn smell of naked sleep under the ceiling fan—Shoved him over on his stomach kicking with slow pleasure—

"Hooded dead gibber in the turnstile—What used to be me is backward sound track—fossil orgasm kneeling to inane cooperation." wind through the pissoir—"*J'aime ces types vicieux qu'ici montrent la bite*"—green place by the water pipe—dead leaves caught in pubic hairs—"Come and jack off—1929"—Woke in stale smell of vending machines—The boy with grey flannel pants stood there grinning a few inches in his hand—Shadow cars and wind through other flesh—came to World's End. Brief boy on screen revolving lips and pants and forgotten hands in countries of the world—

On the sea wall met a boy in red-and-white T-shirt under a circling albatross—"Me Brown Meester?"—warm rain on the iron roof—The boy peeled his stale underwear—Identical erection flipped out in kerosene lamp—The boy jumped on the bed, slapped his thighs: "I screw Johnny up ass? *Así como perros*"—Rectums merging to idiot Mambo—one boy naked in Panama dawn wind—

In the hyacinths the Green Boys smile—Rotting music trailing vines and birdcalls through remote dreamy lands —The initiate awoke in that stale summer dawn smell, suitcases all open on a brass bed in Mexico—In the shower a Mexican about twenty, rectums naked, smell of carbolic soap and barrack toilets—

Trails my summer dawn wind in other flesh strung together on scar impressions of young Panama night—pictures exploded in the kerosene lamp—open shirt flapping in the pissoir—cock flipped out and up—water from his face—sex tingled in the boy's slender tight ass—

"You wanta screw me?"

"Breathe in, Johnny—Here goes—"

They was ripe for the plucking forgot way back yonder in the corn hole—lost in little scraps of delight and burning scrolls—through the open window trailing swamp smells and old newspapers—rectums naked in whiffs of raw meat—genital smells of the two bodies merge in shared meals and belches of institution cooking—spectral smell of empty condoms down along penny arcades and mirrors—Forgotten shadow actor walks beside you—mountain wind of Saturn in the morning sky—From the death trauma weary good-by then—orgasm addicts stacked in the attic like muttering burlap—

Odor rockets over oily lagoons—silver flakes fall through a maze of dirty pictures—windy city outskirts—Smell of empty condoms, excrement, black dust—ragged pants to the ankle—

Bone faces—place of nettles along adobe walls open shirts flapping—savanna and grass mud—The sun went—The mountain shadow touched ragged pants—whisper of dark street in faded Panama photo—"Muy got good one, Meester" smiles through the pissoir—Orgasm siphoned back street smells and a Mexican boy—Woke in the filtered green light, thistle shadows cutting stale underwear—

The three boys lay on the bank rubbing their stomachs against the warm sand—They stood up undressing to swim—Billy gasped as his pants dropped and his cock flipped out he hadn't realized it was that far up from the rubbing—They swam lazily letting the warm water move between their legs and Lloyd walked back to his pants and brought a piece of soap and they passed it back and forth laughing and rubbing each other and Billy ejaculated his thin brown stomach arched out of the water as the spurts shot up in the sunlight like tiny rockets—He sagged down into the water panting and lay there against the muddy bottom—

Under the old trestle trailing vines in the warm summer afternoon undressing to swim and rubbing their bellies—Lloyd rubbing his hand down further and further openly rubbing his crotch now and grinning as the other two watched and Billy looked at Jammy hesitantly and began to rub too and slowly Jammy did the same—They came into the water watching the white blobs drift away—The Mexican boy dropped his pants and his cock flipped out and he looked at Billy grinning—Billy turned and waded into the water and the Mexican followed him and turned him around feeling his crotch and shoved him down on his back in the shallow water, hitched his brown arms under Billy's knees and shoved them back against his chest—The Mexican held his knees with one arm and with the other hand dipped a piece of soap in the water and began rubbing it up and down Billy's ass—Billy shuddered and his body went limp letting it happen—The Mexican was rubbing soap on his own cock now with one hand—shiny black pubic hairs reflected sharp as wire—Slowly shoved his cock in—Billy gasped and moved with it—Spurts fell against his chest in the sunlight and he lay there in the water breathing sewage smells of the canal—

Billy squirmed up onto a muddy bank and took a handful of the warm mud and packed it around his cock and Lloyd poured a bucket of water on the mud and Billy's cock flipped out jumping in the green filtered light under the old trestle—

Stale underwear of penny arcades slipping down legs, rectums feeling the warm sun, laughing and washing each other soapy hands in his crotch, pearly spasms stirring the warm water—whiff of dried jissom in the bandanna trailing sweet young breath through remote lands—soft globs on a brass bed in Mexico—naked—wet—carbolic soap—tight nuts—piece of soap in the locker room rubbing each other off to "My Blue Heaven"—grinning as the other two watched—

The Mexican dropped his pants with a wriggle and stood naked in the filtered green light, vines on his back —Rubbing his crotch now into Billy's ass—Billy moved with it, rectum wriggling cock inside rubbing—

Ali squirmed teeth bared grinning—His thin brown stomach hit the pallet—"You is coming, Johnny?"—Sunlight on the army blankets—rectum wriggling slow fuck on knees "*así como perros*"—orgasm crackled with electric afternoon—bodies stuck together in magnetic eddies—Squirming cock in his intestines, rectum wriggling felt the hot sperm deep in his body—

Shoved him over on his stomach kicking—The Mexican held his knees—Hand dipped a piece of soap—Shoved his cock in laughing—Bodies stuck together in the sunlight kicked whiffs of rectal mucus—laughing teeth and pepper smells—"You is feeling the hot quick Mexican kid naked Mambo to your toes Johnny. . . dust in bare leg hairs tight brown nuts breech very hot . . .How long you want us to fuck very nice Meester? Flesh diseased dirty pictures we fucking tired of fuck very nice Mister." Sad image of sickness at the attic window say something to you "*adios*" worn out film washed back in prep school clothes to distant closing dormitory fragments off the page stained toilet pictures blurred rotting pieces of "Freckle Leg" dormitory dawn dripping water on his face diseased voice so painful telling you "Sparks" is over New York. "Have I done the job here?" With a telescope you can watch our worn out film dim jerky far away shut a bureau drawer faded sepia smile from an old calendar falling leaves sun cold on a thin boy with freckles folded away in an old file now standing last review.

"Maze of dirty pictures and vending machine flesh whispers use of fraud on faded photo—IBM song yodels dime a dozen type overcoats—Not taking any adolescent on shit envelope in the bath cubicle—Come of your stale movies sings Danny Deever in drag—Times lost or strayed long empty cemetery with a moldy pawn ticket —fading whisper down skid row to Market Street shows all kinds masturbation and self-abuse—Young boys need it special." silver paper in the wind distant 1920 wind and dust. He was looking at some thing a long time ago where the second hand book shop used to be just opposite the old cemetery.

"Who? *Quién es?—Hable, señor*—Talk loud and clear."

"We are all from the American women with a delicate lilt—I represent the lithe aloof young men of the breed charmingly—We are all empowered to make arrests and enough with just the right shade of show you."

"*Belt Her*—Find a time buyer before ports are now ended—These are rotten if they start job for instance —Blind bargain in return for accepting 'one more chance'—Generous?—Nothing—That far to the bait and it's curtains—Know what they meant if they start job for instance?"

"Dead young flesh in stale underwear vending sex words to magnetic Law 334—Indicates simple tape is served sir, through iron repetition—Ass and genitals tingling in 1929 jack-off spelt out broken wings of

Icarus—Control system ousted from half the body whispers skin instructions to memory of melting ice—area of Spain—channels ahead loud and clear—Line of the body fitted to other underwear and Kiki steps forward on faded photo—sad image dusted by the Panama night."

"So think before they can do any locks over the Chinese that abolition is war of the past—The end of hanging generous? Just the same position—Changed place of years in the end is just the same—Going to do?—Perhaps alone would you? All good things come to about that was that—"

Call through remote dawn of back yards and ash pits—plaintive ghost in the turnstile—Shadow cars and wind faces came to World's End—street light on soiled clothes dim jerky far away dawn in his eyes. Do you begin to see there is no boy there in the dark room? He was looking at something a long time ago. Changed place?—Same position—Sad image circulates through backward time—Clom Fliday."

Case of the Celluloid Kali

THE NAME IS Clem Snide—I am a Private Ass Hole—I will take on any job any identity any body—I will do anything difficult dangerous or downright dirty for a price—

The man opposite me didn't look like much—A thin grey man in a long coat that flickered like old film—He just happens to be the biggest operator in any time universe—

"I don't care myself you understand"—He watched the ash spiraling down from the end of his Havana—It hit the floor in a puff of grey dust—

"Just like that—Just time—Just time—Don't care myself if the whole fucking shithouse goes up in chunks—I've sat out novas before—I was born in a nova."

"Well Mr. Martin, I guess that's what birth is you might say."

"I wouldn't say—Have to be moving along any case —The ticket that exploded posed little time—Point is they are trying to cross me up—small timers—still on the old evacuation plan—Know what the old evacuation plan is, Mr. Snide?"

"Not in detail."

"The hanging gimmick—death in orgasm—gills—No bones and elementary nervous system—evacuation to the Drenched Lands—a bad deal on the level and it's not on the level with Sammy sitting in—small timers trying to cross me up—Me, Bradly-Martin, who invented the double-cross—Step right up—Now you see me now you don't—A few scores to settle before I travel —a few things to tidy up and that's where you come in—I want you to contact the Venus Mob, the Vegetable People and spill the whole fucking compost heap through Times Square and Piccadilly—I'm not taking any rap for that green bitch—I'm going to rat on everybody and split this dead whistle stop planet wide open —I'm clean for once with the nova heat—like clean fall out—"

He faded in spiraling patterns of cigar smoke—There was a knock at the door—Registered letter from Antwerp—Ten thousand dollar check for film rights to a novel I hadn't written called *The Soft Ticket*—Letter from somebody I never heard of who is acting as my agent suggests I contact the Copenhagen office to discuss the Danish rights on my novel *Expense Account*—

bar backed by pink shell—new Orleans jazz thin in the Northern night. A boy slid off a white silk bar stool and held out the hand: "Hello, I'm Johnny Yen, a friend of—well, just about everybody. I was more physical before my accident you can see from this interesting picture. Only the head was reduced to this jelly but like I say it the impression on my face was taken by the other man's eyes drive the car head-on it was and the Big Physician (he's very technical) rushed him off to a surgery and took out his eyes and made a quick impression and slapped it on me like a pancake before I started to dry out and curl around the edges. So now I'm back in harness you might say: and I have all of 'you' that what I want from my audience is the last drop then bring me another. The place is hermetic. We think so blockade we thought nobody could get thru our flak thing. they thought. Switch Artist me. Oh, there goes my frequency. I'm on now. . ."

The lights dimmed and Johnny pranced out in goggles flickering Northern Lights wearing a jockstrap of undifferentiated tissue that must be in constant movement to avoid crystallization. A penis rose out of the jock and dissolved in pink light back to a clitoris, balls retract into cunt with a fluid plop. Three times he did this to wild "*Olés!*" from the audience. Drifted to the bar and ordered a heavy blue drink. D noted patches of white crystal formed along the scar lines on Johnny's copy face.

"Just like canals. Maybe I'm a Martian when the Crystals are down."

You will die there a screwdriver through the head. The thought like looking at me over steak and explain it all like that stay right here. She was also a Reichian analyst. Disappear more or less remain in acceptable form to you the face.

"We could go on cutting my cleavage act, but *genug basta assez* dice fall *hombre* long switch street. . . I had this terrible accident in a car a Bentley it was I think they're so nice that's what you pay for when you buy one it's yours and you can be sure nobody will pull it out from under our assets. Of course we don't have assholes here you understand somebody might go and get physical. So we are strictly from urine. And that narrows things to a fine line down the middle fifty feefty and what could be fairer than that my Uncle Eyetooth always says he committed fornication but I don't believe it me old heavy water junky like him. . . So anyhoo to get back to my accident in my Bentley once I get my thing in a Bentley it's mine already.

So we had this terrible accident or rather he did. Oh dear what am I saying? It wasn't my first accident you understand yearly wounded or was it monthly Oh dear I must stay on that middle line. . .

"Survivor. Survivor. Not the first in my childhood. Three thousand years in show business and always keep my nose clean. Why I was a dancing boy for the Cannibal Trog Women in the Ice Age. remember? All that meat stacked up in the caves and the Blue Queen covered with limestone flesh creeps into your bones like cold grey honey. . .that's the way they keep them not dead but paralyzed with this awful stuff they cook down from vampire bats get in your hair Gertie always keep your hair way up inside with a vampire on premises bad to get in other alien premises. The Spanish have this word for it, something about props *ajeno* or something like that I know so am *ya la yo* mixa everything allup. They call me Puto the Cement Mixer, now isn't that cute? Some people think I'm just silly but I'm not silly at all. . .and this boyfriend told me I looked just like a shrew ears quivering hot and eager like burning leaves and those were his last words engraved on my back tape—along with a lot of other old memories that disgust me, you wouldn't believe the horrible routines I been involved through my profession of Survival Artist . . .and they think that's funny, but I don't laugh except real quick between words no time you understand laughing they could get at me doesn't keep them off like talking does, now watch—"

A flicker pause and the light shrank and the audience sound a vast muttering in Johnny's voice.

"You see"—Shadows moved back into nightclub seats and drank nightclub drinks and talked nightclub talk—"They'd just best is all. So I was this dancing boy for these dangerous old cunts paralyzed men and boys they dug special stacked right up to the ceiling like the pictures I saw of Belsen or one of those awful contracted places and I said they are at it again. . .I said the Old Army Game. I said 'Pass the buck.' Now you see it, now you don't. . . Paralyzed with this awful gook the Sapphire Goddess let out through this cold sore she always kept open on her lips, that is a hole in the limestone you understand she was like entirely covered with one of those stag rites. . . Real concentrated in there and irradiated to prevent an accident owing to some virus come lately wander in from Podunk Hepatitis. . . But I guess I'm talking too much about private things. . . But I know this big atomic professor, he's very technical too, says: 'There are no secrets any more, Pet,' when I was smooching around him for a quickie. My Uncle still gives me a sawski for a hot nuclear secret and ten years isn't hay, dahling, in these times when practically anybody is subject to wander in from the desert with a quit claim deed and snatch a girl's snatch right out from under her assets. . .over really I should say but some of we boys are so sick we got this awful cunt instead of a decent human asshole disgust you to see it. . . So I just say anything I hear on the old party line.

"I used to keep those old Cave Cunts at bay with my Impersonation Number where I play this American Mate Dance in Black Widow drag and I could make my face flap around you wouldn't believe it and the noises I made in uh orgasm when SHE ate me—I played both parts you unnerstand, imitated the Goddess Herself and turn right into stone for security. . . And SHE couldn't give me enough juice running out of this hole was her only orifice and she was transported dais and all, die ass and all, by blind uniques with no balls, had to crawl under HER dais dressed in Centipede Suit of the Bearer which was put on them as a great honor and they was always fighting over matter of crawl protocol or protocrawl. . . So all these boys stacked to the ceiling covered with limestone. . .you understand they weren't dead any more than a fresh oyster is dead, but died in the moment when the shell was cracked and they were eaten all quivering sweet and tasty. vitamins the right way. . .eaten with little jeweled adzes jade and sapphires and chicken blood rubies all really magnificent. Of course I pinched everything I could latch onto with my prehensile piles I learned it boosting in Chi to pay the Luxury Tax on C. three thousand years in show business. . . Later or was it earlier, the Mayan Calendar is all loused up you know. . . I was a star Corn God inna Sacred Hanging Ceremony to fructify the Corn devised by this impresario who specializes in these far out bit parts which fit me like a condom, he says the cutest things. He's a doctor too. A big physician made my face over after 'the accident' collided with my Bentley head on. . .the cops say they never see anything so intense and it is a special pass I must be carrying I wasn't completely obliterated.

"Oh there's my doctor made the face over after my accident. He calls me Pygmalion now, isn't that cute? You'll love him."

The doctor was sitting in a surgical chair of gleaming nickel. His soft boneless head was covered with grey green fuzz, the right side of his face an inch lower than the left side swollen smooth as a boil around a dead, cold undersea eye.

"Doctor, I want you to meet my friend Mister D the Agent, and he's a lovely fellow too.

("Some time he don't hardly hear what you saying. He's very technical.")

The doctor reached out his abbreviated fibrous fingers in which surgical instruments caught neon and cut Johnny's face into fragments of light.

"Jelly," the doctor said, liquid gurgles through his hardened purple gums. His tongue was split and the two sections curled over each other as he talked: "Life jelly. It sticks and grows on you like Johnny."

Little papules of tissue were embedded in the doctor's hands. The doctor pulled a scalpel out of Johnny's ear and trimmed the papules into an ash tray where they stirred slowly exuding a green juice.

"They say his prick didn't synchronize at all so he cut it off and made some kinda awful cunt between the two sides of him. He got a whole ward full of his 'fans' he call them already.

"When the wind is right you can hear them scream in Town Hall Square. And everybody says 'But this is interesting.'

"I was more *physical* before my *accident,* you can see from this interesting picture."

Lee looked from the picture to the face, saw the flickering phosphorescent scars—

"Yes," he said, "I know you—You're dead *nada* walking around visible."

So the boy is rebuilt and gives me the eye and there he is again walking around some day later across the street and "No dice" flickered across his face—The copy there is a different being, something ready to slip in—

boys empty and banal as sunlight her way always—So he is exact replica is he not?—empty space of the original—

So I tailed the double to London on the Hook Von Holland and caught him out strangling a naked faggot in the bed sitter—I slip on the antibiotic hand cuffs and we adjourn to the Mandrake Club for an informative little chat—

"What do you get out of this?" I ask bluntly.

"A smell I always feel when their eyes pop out"—The boy looked at me his mouth a little open showing the whitest teeth this Private Eye ever saw—naval uniform buttoned in the wrong holes quilted with sea mist and powder smoke, smell of chlorine, rum and moldy jockstraps—and probably a narcotics agent is hiding in the spare stateroom that is always locked—There are the stairs to the attic room he looked out of and his mother moving around—dead she was they say—dead—with such hair too—red.

"Where do you feel it?" I prodded.

"All over," he said, eyes empty and banal as sunlight—"Like hair sprouting all over me"—He squirmed and giggled and creamed in his dry goods—

"And after every job I get to see the movies—You know—" And he gave me the sign twisting his head to the left and up—

So I gave him the sign back and the words jumped in my throat all there like and ready the way they always do when I'm right "You make the pilgrimage?"

"Yes—The road to Rome."

I withdrew the antibiotics and left him there with that dreamy little-boy look twisting the napkin into a hangman's knot—On the bus from the air terminal a thin grey man sat down beside me—I offered him a cigarette and he said "Have one of mine," and I see he is throwing the tin on me—"Nova police—You are Mr. Snide I believe." And he moved right in and shook me down looking at pictures, reading letters checking back on my time track.

"There's one of them," I heard some one say as he looked at a photo in my files.

"Hummm—yes—and here's another—Thank you Mr. Snide—You have been most cooperative—"

I stopped off in Bologna to look up my old friend Green Tony thinking he could probably give me a line —up four flights in a tenement past the old bitch selling black-market cigarettes and cocaine cut with Saniflush, through a dirty brown curtain and there is Green Tony in a pad with Chinese jade all over and Etruscan cuspidors—He is sitting back with his leg thrown over an Egyptian throne smoking a cigarette in a carved emerald holder—He doesn't get up but he says: "Dick Tracy in the flesh," and motions to a Babylonian couch.

I told him what I was after and his face went a bright green with rage, "That stupid bitch—She bringa the heat on all of us—Nova heat—" He blew a cloud of smoke and it hung there solid in front of him—Then he wrote an address in the smoke—"No. 88 Via di Nile, Roma."

This 88 Nile turned out to be one of those bar-soda

fountains like they have in Rome—You are subject to find a maraschino cherry in your dry martini and right next to some citizen is sucking a banana split disgust you to see it—Well I am sitting there trying not to see it so I look down at the far end of the counter and dug a boy very dark with kinky hair and something Abyssinian in his face—Our eyes lock and I give him the sign—And he gives it right back—So I spit the maraschino cherry in the bartender's face and slip him a big tip and he says "*Rivideci* and bigger."

And I say "Up yours with a double strawberry phosphate."

The boy finishes his Pink Lady and follows me out and I take him back to my trap and right away get into an argument with the clerk about no visitors *stranezza* to the hotel—Enough garlic on his breath to deter a covey of vampires—I shove a handful of lire into his mouth "Go buy yourself some more gold teeth," I told him—

When this boy peeled off the dry goods he gives off a slow stink like a thawing mummy—But his asshole sucked me right in all my experience as a Private Eye never felt anything like it—In the flash bulb of orgasm I see that fucking clerk has stuck his head through the transom for a refill—Well expense account—The boy is lying there on the bed spreading out like a jelly slow tremors running through it and sighs and says: "Almost like the real thing isn't it?"

And I said "I need the time milking," and give him the sign so heavy come near slipping a disk.

"I can see you're one of our own," he said warmly sucking himself back into shape—"Dinner at eight"—He comes back at eight in a souped up Ragazzi and we take off 160 per and scream to stop in front of a villa I can see the Bentleys and Hispano Bear Cats and Stutz Suisses and what not piled up and all the golden youth of Europe is disembarking—"Leave your clothes in the vestibule," the butler tells us and we walk in on a room full of people all naked to a turn sitting around on silk stools and a bar with a pink shell behind it—This cunt undulates forward and give me the sign and holds out her hand "I am the Contessa di Vile your hostess for tonight"—She points to the boys at the bar with her cigarette holder and their cocks jumped up one after the other—And I did the polite thing too when my turn came—

So all the boys began chanting in unison *"The movies! —The movies!*—We want *the movies!—"* So she led the way into the projection room which was filled with pink light seeping through the walls and floor and ceiling—The boy was explaining to me that these were actual films taken during the Abyssinian War and how lucky I was to be there—Then the action starts—There on the screen is a gallows and some young soldiers standing around with prisoners in loincloths—The soldiers are dragging this kid up onto the gallows and he biting and screaming and shitting himself and his loincloth slips off and they shove him under the noose and one of them tightens it around his neck standing there now mother naked—Then the trap fell and he drops kicking and yelping and you could hear his neck snap like a stick in a wet towel—He hangs there pulling his knees up to the chest and pumping out spurts of jissom and the audience coming right with him spurt for spurt —So the soldiers strip the loincloths off the others and they all got hard-ons waiting and watching—Got through a hundred of them more or less one at a time— Then they run the movie in slow motion slower and slower and you are coming slower and slower until it took an hour and then two hours and finally all the boys are standing there like statues getting their rocks off geologic—Meanwhile an angle comes dripping down and forms a stalactite in my brain and I slip back to the projection room and speed up the movie so the hanged boys are coming like machine guns—Half the guests explode straightaway from altered pressure chunks of limestone whistling through the air. The others are flopping around on the floor like beached idiots and the Contessa gasps out "Carbon dioxide for the love of Kali"—So somebody turned on the carbon dioxide tanks and I made it out of there in an aqualung—Next thing the nova heat moves in and bust the whole aquarium.

"Humm, yes, and here's another planet—"

The officer moved back dissolving most cooperative connections formed by the parasite—Self-righteous millions stabbed with rage.

"That bitch—She brings the heat three dimensional."

"The ugly cloud of smoke hung there solid female blighted continent—This turned out to be one of those association locks in Rome—I look down at the end—

He quiets you, remember?—Finis. So I spit the planet from all the pictures and give him a place of residence with inflexible authority—Well, no terms—A hand has been taken—Your name fading looks like—Madison Avenue machine disconnected."

The Mayan Caper

JOE BRUNDIGE BRINGS YOU the shocking story of the Mayan Caper exclusive to *The Evening News*—

A Russian scientist has said: "We will travel not only in space but in time as well"—I have just returned from a thousand-year time trip and I am here to tell you what I saw—And to tell you how such time trips are made—It is a precise operation—It is difficult—It is dangerous—It is the new frontier and only the adventurous need apply—But it belongs to *anyone* who has the courage and know-how to enter—It belongs to *you*—

I started my trip in the morgue with old newspapers, folding in today with yesterday and typing out composites—When you skip through a newspaper as most of us do you see a great deal more than you know—In fact you see it all on a subliminal level—Now when I fold today's paper in with yesterday's paper and arrange the pictures to form a time section montage, I am literally moving back to the time when I read yesterday's paper, that is traveling in time back to yesterday—I did this eight hours a day for three months—I went back as far as the papers went—I dug out old magazines and forgotten novels and letters—I made fold-ins and composites and I did the same with photos—

The next step was carried out in a film studio—I learned to talk and think backward on all levels—This was done by running film and sound track backward—For example a picture of myself eating a full meal was reversed, from satiety back to hunger—First the film was run at normal speed, then in slow-motion—The same procedure was extended to other physiological processes including orgasm—(It was explained to me that I must put aside all sexual prudery and reticence, that sex was perhaps the heaviest anchor holding one in present time.) For three months I worked with the studio—My basic training in time travel was completed and I was now ready to train specifically for the Mayan assignment—

I went to Mexico City and studied the Mayans with a team of archaeologists—The Mayans lived in what is now Yucatan, British Honduras, and Guatemala—I will not recapitulate what is known of their history, but some observations on the Mayan calendar are essential to understanding this report—The Mayan calendar starts from a mythical date 5 Ahua 8 Cumhu and rolls on to the end of the world, also a definite date depicted in the codices as a God pouring water on the earth—The Mayans had a solar, a lunar, and a ceremonial calendar rolling along like interlocking wheels from 5 Ahua 8 Cumhu to the end—The absolute power of the priests, who formed about 2 percent of the population, depended on their control of this calendar—The extent of this number monopoly can be deduced from the fact that the Mayan verbal language contains no number above ten—Modern Mayan-speaking Indians use Spanish numerals—Mayan agriculture was of the slash and burn type—They had no plows. Plows can not be used in the Mayan area because there is a strata of limestone six inches beneath the surface and the slash and burn method is used to this day—Now slash and burn agriculture is a matter of precise timing—The brush must be cut at a certain time so it will have time to dry and the burning operation carried out before the rains start—A few days' miscalculation and the year's crop is lost—

The Mayan writings have not been fully deciphered, but we know that most of the hieroglyphs refer to dates in the calendar, and these numerals have been translated—It is probable that the other undeciphered symbols refer to the ceremonial calendar—There are only three Mayan codices in existence, one in Dresden, one in Paris, one in Madrid, the others having been burned by Bishop Landa—Mayan is very much a living language and in the more remote villages nothing else is spoken—More routine work—I studied Mayan and listened to it on the tape recorder and mixed Mayan in with English—I made innumerable photomontages of Mayan codices and artifacts—the next step was to find a "vessel"—We sifted through many candidates before settling on a young Mayan worker recently arrived from Yucatan—This boy was about twenty, almost black, with the sloping forehead and curved nose of the ancient Mayans—(The physical type has undergone little alteration)—He was illiterate—He had a history of epilepsy—He was what mediums call a "sensitive"—For another three months I worked with the boy on the tape recorder mixing his speech with mine—(I was quite fluent in Mayan at this point—Unlike Aztec it is an easy language.) It was time now for "the transfer operation"—"I" was to be moved into the body of this young Mayan—The operation is illegal and few are competent to practice it—I was referred to an American doctor who had become a heavy metal addict and lost his certificate—"He is the best transfer artist in the industry" I was told "For a price."

We found the doctor in a dingy office on the Avenida Cinco de Mayo—He was a thin grey man who flickered in and out of focus like an old film—I told him what I wanted and he looked at me from a remote distance without warmth or hostility or any emotion I had ever experienced in myself or seen in another—He nodded silently and ordered the Mayan boy to strip, and ran practiced fingers over his naked body—The doctor picked up a box-like instrument with electrical attachments and moved it slowly up and down the boy's back from the base of the spine to the neck—The instrument clicked like a Geiger counter—The doctor sat down and explained to me that the operation was usually performed with "the hanging technique"—The patient's neck is broken and during the orgasm that results he passes into the other body—This method, however, was obsolete and dangerous—For the operation to succeed you must work with a pure vessel who has not been subject to parasite invasion—Such subjects are almost impossible to find in present time he stated flatly—His cold grey eyes flicked across the young Mayan's naked body:

"This subject is riddled with parasites—If I were to employ the barbarous method used by some of my learned colleagues—(nameless assholes)—you would be eaten body and soul by crab parasites—My technique is quite different—I operate with molds—Your body will remain here intact in deepfreeze—On your return, if you do return, you can have it back." He looked pointedly at my stomach sagging from sedentary city life—"You could do with a stomach tuck, young man—But one thing at a time—The transfer operation will take some weeks—And I warn you it will be expensive."

I told him that cost was no object—The *News* was behind me all the way—He nodded briefly: "Come back at this time tomorrow." When we returned to the doctor's office he introduced me to a thin young man who had the doctor's cool removed grey eyes—"This is my photographer—I will make my molds from his negatives." The photographer told me his name was Jiminez

—("Just call me 'Jimmy the Take' ")—We followed the "Take" to a studio in the same building equipped with a 35 millimeter movie camera and Mayan backdrops—He posed us naked in erection and orgasm, cutting the images in together down the middle line of our bodies—Three times a week we went to the doctor's office—He looked through rolls of film his eyes intense, cold, impersonal—And ran the clicking box up and down our spines—Then he injected a drug which he described as a variation of the apomorphine formula—The injection caused simultaneous vomiting and orgasm and several times I found myself vomiting and ejaculating in the Mayan vessel—The doctor told me these exercises were only the preliminaries and that the actual operation, despite all precautions and skills, was still dangerous enough.

At the end of three weeks he indicated the time has come to operate—He arranged us side by side naked on the operating table under floodlights—With a phosphorescent pencil he traced the middle line of our bodies from the cleft under the nose down to the rectum —Then he injected a blue fluid of heavy cold silence as word dust fell from demagnetized patterns—From a remote Polar distance I could see the doctor separate the two halves of our bodies and fitting together a composite being—I came back in other flesh the lookout different, thoughts and memories of the young Mayan drifting through my brain—

The doctor gave me a bottle of the vomiting drug which he explained was efficacious in blocking out any control waves—He also gave me another drug which, if injected into a subject, would enable me to occupy his body for a few hours and only at night. "Don't let the sun come up on you or it's curtains—zero eaten by crab—And now there is the matter of my fee."

I handed him a brief case of bank notes and he faded into the shadows furtive and seedy as an old junky.

The paper and the embassy had warned me that I would be on my own, a thousand years from any help—I had a vibrating camera gun sewed into my fly, a small tape recorder and a transistor radio concealed in a clay pot—I took a plane to Mérida where I set about contacting a "broker" who could put me in touch with a "time guide"—Most of these so-called "brokers" are old drunken frauds and my first contact was no exception—I had been warned to pay nothing until I was satisfied with the arrangements—I found this "broker" in a filthy hut on the outskirts surrounded by a rubbish heap of scrap iron, old bones, broken pottery and worked flints—I produced a bottle of *aguardiente* and the broker immediately threw down a plastic cup of the raw spirit and sat there swaying back and forth on a stool while I explained my business—He indicated that what I wanted was extremely difficult—Also dangerous and illegal—He could get into trouble—Besides I might be an informer from the Time Police—He would have to think about it—He drank two more cups of spirit and fell on the floor in a stupor—The following day I called again—He had thought it over and perhaps—In any case he would need a week to prepare his medicines and this he could only do if he were properly supplied with *aguardiente*—And he poured another glass of spirits slopping full—Extremely dissatisfied with the way things were going I left—As I was walking back toward town a boy fell in beside me.

"Hello, Meester, you look for broker yes?—Muy know good one—Him," he gestured back toward the hut. "No good *borracho* son bitch bastard—Take *mucho dinero*—No do nothing—You come with me, Meester."

Thinking I could not do worse, I accompanied the boy to another hut built on stilts over a pond—A youngish man greeted us and listened silently while I explained what I wanted—The boy squatted on the floor rolling a marijuana cigarette—He passed it around and we all smoked—The broker said yes he could make the arrangements and named a price considerably lower than what I had been told to expect—How soon?—He looked at a shelf where I could see a number of elaborate hourglasses with sand in different colors: red, green, black, blue, and white—The glasses were marked with symbols—He explained to me that the sand represented color time and color words—He pointed to a symbol on the green glass,"Then—One hour"—He took out some dried mushrooms and herbs and began cooking them in a clay pot—As green sand touched the symbol, he filled little clay cups and handed one to me and one to the boy—I drank the bitter medicine and almost immediately the pictures I had seen of Mayan artifacts and codices began moving in my brain like animated cartoons—A spermy, compost heap smell filled the room—The boy began to twitch and mutter and fell to the floor in a fit—I could see that he had an erection under his thin trousers—The broker opened the boy's shirt and pulled off his pants—The penis flipped out spurting in orgasm after orgasm—A green light filled the room and burned through the boy's flesh—Suddenly he sat up talking in Mayan—The words curled out his mouth and hung visible in the air like vine tendrils—I felt a strange vertigo which I recognized as the motion sickness of time travel—The broker smiled and held out a hand—I passed over his fee—The boy was putting on his clothes—He beckoned me to follow and I got up and left the hut—We were walking along a jungle hut the boy ahead his whole body alert and twitching like a dog—We walked many hours and it was dawn when we came to a clearing where I could see a number of workers with sharp sticks and gourds of seed planting corn—The boy touched my shoulder and disappeared up the path in jungle dawn mist—

As I stepped forward into the clearing and addressed one of the workers, I felt the crushing weight of evil insect control forcing my thoughts and feelings into prearranged molds, squeezing my spirit in a soft invisible vise—The worker looked at me with dead eyes empty of curiosity or welcome and silently handed me a planting stick—It was not unusual for strangers to wander in out of the jungle since the whole area was ravaged by soil exhaustion—So my presence occasioned no comment—I worked until sundown—I was assigned to a hut by an overseer who carried a carved stick and wore an elaborate headdress indicating his rank—I lay down in the hammock and immediately felt stabbing probes of telepathic interrogation—I turned on the thoughts of a half-witted young Indian—After some hours the invisible presence withdrew—I had passed the first test—

During the months that followed I worked in the fields—The monotony of this existence made my disguise as a mental defective quite easy—I learned that one could be transferred from field work to rock carving the stellae after a long apprenticeship and only after the priests were satisfied that any thought of resistance was forever extinguished—I decided to retain the anonymous status of a field worker and keep as far as possible out of notice—

A continuous round of festivals occupied our evenings and holidays—On these occasions the priests appeared in elaborate costumes, often disguised as centipedes or lobsters—Sacrifices were rare, but I witnessed one revolting ceremony in which a young captive was tied to a stake and the priests tore his sex off with white-hot copper claws—I learned also something of the horrible punishments meted out to anyone who dared challenge or even think of challenging the controllers: *Death in the Ovens:* The violator was placed in a construction of interlocking copper grills—The grills were then heated to white heat and slowly closed on his body. *Death In Centipede:* The "criminal" was strapped to a couch and eaten alive by giant centipedes—These executions were carried out secretly in rooms under the temple.

I made recordings of the festivals and the continuous music like a shrill insect frequency that followed the workers all day in the fields—However, I knew that to play these recordings would invite immediate detection—I needed not only the sound track of control but the image track as well before I could take definitive action—I have explained that the Mayan control system depends on the calendar and the codices which contain symbols representing all states of thought and feeling possible to human animals living under such limited circumstances—These are the instruments with which they rotate and control units of thought—I found out also that the priests themselves do not understand exactly how the system works and that I undoubtedly knew more about it than they did as a result of my intensive training and studies—The technicians who had devised the control system had died out and the present line of priests were in the position of some one who knows what buttons to push in order to set a machine in motion, but would have no idea how to fix that machine if it broke down, or to construct another if the machine were destroyed—If I could gain access to the codices and mix the sound and image track the priests would go on pressing the old buttons with unexpected results—In order to accomplish the purpose I prostituted myself to one of the priests—(Most distasteful thing I ever stood still for)—During the sex act he metamorphosed himself into a green crab from the waist up, retaining human legs and genitals that secreted a caustic erogenous slime, while a horrible stench filled the hut—I was able to endure these horrible encounters by promising myself the pleasure of killing this disgusting monster when the time came—And my reputation as an idiot was by now so well established that I escaped all but the most routine control measures—

The priest had me transferred to janitor work in the temple where I witnessed some executions and saw the prisoners torn body and soul into writhing insect fragments by the ovens, and learned that the giant centipedes were born in the ovens from these mutilated screaming fragments—It was time to act—Using the drug the doctor had given me, I took over the priest's body, gained access to the room where the codices were kept, and photographed the books—Equipped now with sound and image track of the control machine I was in position to dismantle it—I had only to mix the order of recordings and the order of images and the changed order would be picked up and fed back into the machine—I had recordings of all agricultural operations, cutting and burning brush etc.—I now correlated the recordings of burning brush with the image track of this operation, and shuffled the time so that the order to burn came late and a year's crop was lost—Famine weakening control lines, I cut radio static into the control music and festival recordings together with sound and image track rebellion.

"Cut word lines—Cut music lines—Smash the control

images—Smash the control machine—Burn the books—Kill the priests—Kill! Kill! Kill!—"

Inexorably as the machine had controlled thought feeling and sensory impressions of the workers, the machine now gave the order to dismantle itself and kill the priests—I had the satisfaction of seeing the overseer pegged out in the field, his intestines perforated with hot planting sticks and crammed with corn—I broke out my camera gun and rushed the temple—This weapon takes and vibrates image to radio static—You see the priests *were* nothing but word and image, an old film rolling on and on with dead actors—Priests and temple guards went up in silver smoke as I blasted my way into the control room and burned the codices—Earthquake tremors under my feet I got out of there fast, blocks of limestone raining all around me—A great weight fell from the sky, winds of the earth whipping palm trees to the ground—Tidal waves rolled over the Mayan control calendar.

I Sekuin

THE MAYAN CAPER—THE CENTIPEDE SWITCH—THE HEAVY METAL GIMMICK.

I Sekuin, perfected these arts along the streets of Minraud. Under sign of the Centipede. A captive head. In Minraud time. In the tattoo booths. The flesh graft parlors. Living wax works of Minraud. Saw the dummies made to impression. While you wait. From short-time. In the terminals of Minraud. Saw the white bug juice spurt from ruptured spines. In the sex rooms of Minraud. While you wait. In Minraud time. The sex devices of flesh. The centipede penis. Insect hairs thru grey-purple flesh. Of the scorpion people. The severed heads. In tanks of sewage. Eating green shit. In the aquariums of Minraud. The booths of Minraud. Under sign of the centipede. The sex rooms and flesh films of Minraud. I Sekuin a captive head. Learned the drugs of Minraud. In flak Braille. Rot brain and spine. Leave a crab body broken on the brass and copper street. I Sekuin captive head. Carried thru the booths of Minraud. By arms. Legs.

Extensions. From the flesh works of Minraud. My head in a crystal sphere of heavy fluid. Under sing sign of the scorpion goddess. Captive in Minraud. In the time booths of Minraud. In the tattoo parlors of Minraud. In the flesh works of Minraud. In the sex rooms of Minraud. In the flesh films of Minraud. March my captive head. HER captive in Minraud time streets.

On a level plain in the dry sound of insect wings Bradly crash landed a yellow cub—area of painted booths and vacant lots—in a dusty shopwindow of trusses and plaster feet, a severed head on sand, red ants crawling through nose and lips—

"You crazy or something walk around alone?"

The guide pointed to the head: "Guard—You walk through his eyes and you N.G." The guide sliced a hand across his genitals: "This bad place, Meester—You *ven conmigo*—"

He led the way through dusty streets—Metal excrement glowed in corners—Darkness fell in heavy chunks blocking out sections of the city.

"Here," said the guide—"A restaurant cut from limestone, green light seeping through bottles and tanks where crustaceans moved in slow gyrations—The waiter took their order hissing cold dank breath through a disk mouth.

"Good place—cave crabs—*Muy bueno* for fuck, Johnny—"

The waiter set down a flat limestone shell of squid bodies with crab claws.

"Krishnus," said the guide.

Still alive, moving faintly in phosphorescent slime—The guide speared one on a bamboo spike and dipped it into yellow sauce—A sweet metal taste burned through stomach intestines and genitals—Bradly ate the krishnus in ravenous gulps—

The guide raised his arm from the elbow, "*Muy bueno*, Johnny—You see." The waiter was singing through his disk mouth a bubbling cave song—"*Vámanos*, Johnny—I show you good place—We smoke fuck sleep O.K. Muy got good one, Johnny—"

Word "Hotel" exploded in genitals—An old junky took Bradly's money and led them to a blue cubicle—Bradly leaned out a square hole in one wall and saw that the cubicle projected over a void on rusty iron props—The floor moved slightly and creaked under their feet—

"Some time this trap fall—Last fuck for Johnny."

There was a pallet on the iron floor, a brass tray with hashish pipes, and a stone jar.

"Johnny shirt off"—said the guide unbuttoning Bradly's shirt with gentle lush rolling fingers—"Johnny pants down"—He dipped a green phosphorescent

Pretend an Interest

BENWAY "CAMPED" in the Board of Health. He rushed in anywhere brazenly impounding all junk. He was of course well-known but by adroit face rotation managed to piece out the odds, juggling five or six bureaus in the air thin and tenuous drifting-away cobwebs in a cold Spring wind under dead crab eyes of a doorman in green uniform carrying an ambiguous object composite of club, broom and toilet plunger, trailing a smell of ammonia and scrubwoman flesh. An undersea animal surfaced in his face, round disk mouth of cold grey gristle, purple rasp tongue moving in green saliva: "Soul Cracker," Benway decided. Species of carnivorous mollusk. Exists on Venus. It might not have bones. Time-switched the tracks through a field of little white flowers by the ruined signal tower. Sat down under a tree worn smooth by others sat there before. We remember the days as long procession of the Secret Police always everywhere in different form. In Guayaquil sat on the river bank and saw a big lizard cross the mud flats dotted with melon rind from passing canoes.

Carl's dugout turned slowly in the brown iridescent lagoon infested with sting ray, fresh water shark, arequipa, candirus, water boa, crocodile, electric eel, aquatic panther and other noxious creatures dreamed up by the lying explorers who infest bars marginal to the area.

"This inaccessible tribe, you dig, lives on phosphorescent metal paste they mine from the area. Transmute to gold straightaway and shit it out in nuggets. It's the great work."

Liver-sick gold eyes gold maps gold teeth over the *aguardiente* cooked on the Primus stove with canella and tea to cut the oil taste leaves silver sores in the mouth and throat.

"That was the year of the Rindpest when all the tourists died even the Scandinavians and we boys reduced to hawk the farter LWR—Local Wage Rate."

"No calcium in the area you understand. One blighter lost his entire skeleton and we had to carry him about in a canvas bathtub. A jaguar lapped him up in the end, largely for the salt I think."

Tin boys reduced to hawk the farter the substance and the strata—You know what that means? Carried the youth to dead water infested with consent—That was the year of The Clear—Local Wage Rate of Program Empty Body—

"Head Waters of the Baboon-asshole. . . That's hanging vine country—" (The hanging vine flicked around the youth's neck molding to his skull bones in a spiraling tendril motion snapped his neck, he hangs now ejaculating as disk mouths lined with green hairs fasten to his rectum growing tendrils through his body dissolving his bones in liquid gurgles and plops into the green eating jelly.)

"This bad place you write, Meester. You win something like jellyfish."

They live in translucent jelly and converse in light flashes liquefying bones of the world and eating the jelly—boy chrysalis rotting in the sun—lazy undersea eyes on the nod over the rotting meat vegetable sleep—limestone dope out of shale and water. . .

The youth is hanged fresh and bloody—Tall ceremony involves a scorpion head—lethal mating operation from the Purified Ones—No calcium in the area—Exists on Venus—It might not have bones—Ray moss of orgasm and death—Limestone God a mile away—Better than shouts: "Empty body!" Dead land here you understand waiting for some one marginal to the area.

"Deep in fucking drum country" (The naked Initiate is strapped with his back and buttocks fitted to a wooden drum. The drummer beats out orgasm message until the Initiate's flesh lights up with blue flame inside and the drum takes life and fucks the boy ((puffs of smoke across a clear blue sky. . .)) The initiate awoke in other flesh the lookout different. . . And he plopped into squares and patios on "Write me Meester.")

Puerto Joselito is located at the confluence of two strong brown rivers. The town is built over a vast mud flat crisscrossed by stagnant canals, the buildings on stilts joined by a maze of bridges and catwalks extend up from the mud flats into higher ground surrounded by tree columns and trailing lianas, the whole area presenting the sordid and dilapidated air of a declining frontier post or an abandoned carnival.

"The town of Puerto Joselito, dreary enough in its physical aspect, exudes a suffocating fog of smoldering rancid evil as if the town and inhabitants were slowly sinking in wastes and garbage. I found these people deep in the vilest superstitions and practices.

"Various forms of ritual execution are practiced here. These gooks have an aphrodisiac so powerful as to cause death in a total blood spasm leaving the empty body cold and white as marble. This substance is secreted by the Species Xiucutl Crustanus, a flying scorpion, during its lethal mating season in the course of which all male Xiucutl die maddened by the substance and will fly on any male creature infecting with its deadly sperm. In one ceremony the condemned are painted as gold, silver, copper and marble statues, then inoculated with Xiucutl sperm their convulsions are channeled by invisible control wires into exquisite ballets and freeze into garden fountains and park pedestals. And this is one of many ceremonies revolving on the

Ceremonial Calendar kept by the Purified Ones and the Earth Mother.

"The Purified One selects a youth each month and he is walled into a crystal cubicle molded on cervical vertebrae. On the walls of the cubicle, sex programs are cut in cuneiforms and the walls revolve on silent hydraulic pressures. At the end of the month the youth is carried through the street on a flower float and ceremonially hanged in the limestone ball court, it being thought that all human dross passes from the Purified One to die in the youth at the moment of orgasm and death. Before the youth is hanged he must give his public consent, and if he cannot be brought to consent he hangs the Purified One and takes over his functions. The Purified Ones are officially immortal with monthly injections of youth substance." Quote Green-Baum Early Explorer.

Carl's outboard vibrated in a haze of rusty oil, bit a jagged piece out of the dugout canoe and sank, in iridescent brown water. Somewhere in the distance the muffled jelly sound of underwater dynamite: ("The natives are fishing"). howler monkeys like wind through leaves. The dugout twisted slowly and stopped, touching a ruined jetty. Carl got out with his Nordic rucksack and walked to the square on high ground. He felt a touch on his shoulder light as wind. A man in moldy grey police tunic and red flannel underwear one bare foot swollen and fibrous like old wood covered with white fungus, his eyes mahogany color flickered as the watcher moved in and out. He gasped out the word "Control" and slipped to the ground. A man in grey hospital pajamas eating handfuls of dirt and trailing green spit crawled over to Carl and pulled at his pants cuff. Another moves forward on brittle legs breaking little puffs of bone meal. His eyes lit up a stern glare went out in smell of burning metal. From all sides they came pawing hissing spitting: "*Papeles,*" "*Documentes,*" "*Passaport.*"

"What is all this scandal?" The Comandante in clean khaki was standing on a platform overlooking the square. Above him was an elaborate multileveled building of bamboo. His shirt was open on a brown chest smooth as old ivory. A little pistol in red leather cover crawled slowly across his skin leaving an iridescent trail of slime.

"You must forgive my staff if they do not quite measure up to your German ideal of spit and polish. . . backward. . . uninstructed. . . each living all alone and cultivating his little virus patch. . . They have absolutely nothing to do and the solitude. . ." He tapped his forehead. His face melted and changed under the flickering arc lights.

"But there must be thirty of them about," said Carl.

The Comandante gave him a sharp look. "They are synchronized of course. They can not see or even infer each other so all think he is only police officer on post. Their lines you *sabe* never cross and some of them are already. . ."

"And some of them are already dead. This is awkward since they are not legally responsible. We try to bury them on time even if they retain intact protest reflex. Like Gonzalez the Earth Eater. We bury him three times." The Comandante held up three fingers sprouting long white tendrils. "Always he eat way out. And now if you will excuse me the soccer scores are coming in from the Capital. One must pretend an interest."

The Comandante had aged from remote crossroads of Time crawled into a metal locker and shut the door whimpering with fears, emerged in a moldy green jock-strap his body painted I-red, U-green. The Assistant flared out of a broom closet high on ammonia with a green goatee and marble face. He removed Carl's clothes in a series of locks and throws. Carl could feel his body move to the muscle orders. The Assistant put a pail over his head and screamed away into distant hammers.

The Comandante spread jelly over Carl's naked paralyzed body. The Comandante was molding a woman. Carl could feel his body draining into the woman mold. His genitals dissolving, tits swelling as the Comandante penetrated applying a few touches to face and hair—(Jissom across the mud wall in the dawn sound of barking dogs and running water—) Down there the Comandante going through his incantations around Carl's empty body. The body rose presenting an erection, masturbates in front of the Comandante. Penis flesh spreads through his body bursting in orgasm explosions granite cocks ejaculate lava under a black cloud boiling with monster crustaceans. Cold grey undersea eyes and hands touched

Carl's body. The Comandante flipped him over with sucker hands and fastened his disk mouth to Carl's asshole. He was lying in a hammock of green hair, penis-flesh hammers bursting his body. Hairs licked his rectum, spiraling tendrils scraping pleasure centers, Carl's body emptied in orgasm after orgasm, bones lit up green through flesh dissolved into the disk mouth with a fluid plop. He quivers red now in boneless spasms, pink waves through his body at touch of the green hairs.

The Comandante stripped Carl's body and smeared on green jelly nipples that pulled the flesh up and in. Carl's genitals wither to dry shit he sweeps clear with a little whisk broom to white flesh and black shiny pubic hairs. The Comandante parts the hairs and makes Incision with a little curved knife. Now he is modeling a face from the picture of his *novia* in the Capital.

"And now, how you say, 'the sound effects.' " He puts on a record of her voice, Carl's lips follow and the female substance breathed in the words.

"Oh love of my *alma!* Oh wind of morning!"

"Most distasteful thing I ever stand still for." Carl made words in the air without a throat, without a tongue. "I hope there is a *farmacia* in the area."

The Comandante looked at him with annoyance: "You could wait in the office please."

He came out putting on his tunic and strapping on a Luger.

"A drugstore? Yes I *creo*. . . Across the lagoon. . . I will call the guide."

Carl walked through a carnival city along canals where giant pink salamanders and goldfish stirred slowly, penny arcades, tattoo booths, massage parlors, side shows, blue movies, processions, floats, performers, pitchmen to the sky.

Puerto Joselito is located Dead Water. Inactive oil wells and mine shafts, strata of abandoned machinery and gutted boats, garbage of stranded operations and expeditions that died at this point of dead land where sting rays bask in brown water and grey crabs walk the mud flats on brittle stilt legs. The town crops up from the mud flats to the silent temple of high jungle streams of clear water cut deep clefts in yellow clay and falling orchids endanger the traveler.

In a green savanna stand two vast penis figures in black stone, legs and arms vestigial, slow blue smoke rings pulsing from the stone heads. A limestone road winds through the pillars and into The City. A rack of rusty iron and concrete set in vacant lots and rubble, dotted with chemical gardens. A smell of junky hat and death about the town deadens and weight these sentences with "disgust you to see it." Carl walked through footpaths of a vast shanty town. A dry wind blows hot and cold down from Chimborazo a soiled post card in the prop blue sky. Crab men peer out of abandoned quarries and shag heaps some sort of vestigial eye growing cheek bone and a look about them as if they could take root and grow on anybody. muttering addicts of the orgasm drug, boneless in the sun, gurgling throat gristle, heart pulsing slowly in transparent flesh eaten alive by the crab men.

Carl walked through the penis posts into a town of limestone huts. A ring of priests sat around the posts legs spread, erections pulsing to flicker light from their eyes. As he walked through the electric eyes his lips swelled and his lungs rubbed against the soft inner ribs. He walked over and touched one of the priests and a shock threw him across the road into a sewage ditch. Maize fields surround the town with stone figures of the Young Corn God erect penis spurting maize shoots looks down with young cruelty and innocent lips parted slightly terminal caress in the dropping eyes. The Young Corn God is led out and his robes of corn silk stripped from his body by lobster priests. A vine rope is attached to the stone penis of the Maize God. The boy's cock rises iridescent in the morning sun and you can see the other room from there by a mirror on the wardrobe. . . Well now, in the city a group of them came to this valley grow corn do a bit of hunting fishing in the river.

Carl walked a long row of living penis urns made from men whose penis has absorbed the body with vestigial arms and legs breathing through purple fungoid gills and dropping a slow metal excrement like melted solder forms a solid plaque under the urns stand about three feet high on rusty iron shelves wire mesh cubicles joined by catwalks and ladders a vast warehouse of living penis urns slowly transmuting to smooth red terra cotta. Others secrete from the head crystal pearls of lubricant that forms a shell of solid crystal over the red penis flesh.

A blast of golden horns: "The Druid priest emerges from the Sacred Grove, rotting bodies hang about him like Spanish moss. His eyes blue and cold as liquid air expand and contract eating light."

The boy sacrifice is chosen by erection acclaim. universal erection feeling for him until all pricks point to "Yes." Boy feels the "Yes" run through him and melt his bones to "Yes" stripped naked in the Sacred Grove shivering and twitching under the Hanging Tree green disk mouths sucking his last bone meal. He goes to the Tree naked on flower floats through the obsidian streets red stone buildings and copper pagodas of the Fish City stopping in Turkish Baths and sex rooms to make blue movies with youths. The entire city is in heat during this ceremony, faces swollen with tumescent purple penis flesh. Lightning fucks flash on any street corner leave a smell of burning metal blue sparks up and down the spine. A vast bath-town of red clay cubicles over twisting geological orgasm with the green crab boys disk mouths' slow rasping tongues on spine centers twisting in the warm black ooze.

Noteworthy is the Glazing Ceremony when certain of the living urns are covered with terra cotta and baked in red brick ovens by the women who pull the soft red meat out with their penis forks and decorate house and garden with the empty urns. The urnings for the Glazing Ceremony are chosen each day by locker number from the public urn and numbers read out over the soft speaker inside the head. Helpless urns listening to the number call charge our soft terror-eating substance, our rich substance.

Now it is possible to beat the number before call by fixing the urn or after call by the retroactive fix which few are competent to practice. There is also a Ceremonial Massage in which the penis flesh is rubbed in orgasm after orgasm until Death in Centipede occurs. Death in Centipede is the severest sentence of the Insect Court and of course all urnings are awaiting sentence for various male crimes. *Pues,* every year a few experienced urnings beat the house and make Crystal Grade. When the crystal cover reaches a certain thickness the urning is exempt from ceremonial roll call and becomes immortal with nothing to do but slowly accrete a thicker cover in the Crystal Hall of Fame.

Few beat the house. a vast limestone bat. High mountain valley cut off by severest sentence of symbiotic cannibalism. So the game with one another.

"I dunno me. Only work here. Technical Sergeant."

"Throw it into wind Jack."

A pimp leans in through the Country Club window. "Visit the House of David boys and watch the girls eat shit. Makes a man feel good all over. Just tell the madam a personal friend of mine." He drops a cuneiform cylinder into the boy's hip pocket feeling his ass with lost tongue of the penis urn people in a high mountain valley of symbiotic cannibalism. The natives are blond and blue-eyed sex in occupation. It is unlawful to have orgasm alone and the inhabitants live in a hive of sex rooms and flickering blue movie cubicles. You can spot one on the cubicle skyline miles away. We all live in the blue image forever. The cubicles fade out in underground steam baths where lurk the Thurlings, malicious boys' spirits fugitive from the blue movie who mislead into underground rivers. (The traveler is eaten by aquatic centipedes and carnivorous underwater vines.)

Orgasm death spurts over the flower floats—Limestone God a mile away—Descent into penis flesh cut off by a group of them came to this game under the Hanging Tree—Insect legs under red Arctic night—He wore my clothes and terror—

The boy ejaculates blood over the flower floats. Slow vine rope drops him in a phallic fountain. wire mesh cubicles against the soft inner ribs. vast warehouse of penis and the shock threw him ten feet to smooth dirt and flak. God with erect penis spurting crystal young cruelty and foe solid. dazzling terminal caress in silent corridors of Corn God. erection feeling for descent in the morning sun feels the "Yes" from there by a mirror on you stripped naked. In the city a group of them came to this last bone meal under the Hanging Tree.

"Pretty familiar."

The Priests came through the Limestone Gates playing green flutes: translucent lobster men with wild blue eyes and shells of flexible copper. A soundless vibration in the spine touched center of erection and the natives moved toward the flute notes on a stiffening blood tube for the Centipede Rites. A stone penis body straddles the opening to the cave room of steam baths and sex cubicles and the green cab boys who go all the way on any line.

The Natives insert a grill of silver wires deep into the sinus where a crystal slowly forms. They strum the wires with insect hairs growing through flesh weaving cold cocaine sex frequencies.

From The Living God Cock flows a stream of lubricant into a limestone trough green with algae. The priests arrange the initiates into long dog-fuck lines molding them together with green jelly from the lubricant tanks. Now the centipede skin is strapped on each body a segment and the centipede whips and cracks in electric spasms of pleasure throwing off segments kicking spasmodically uncontrolled diarrhea spurting orgasm after orgasm synchronized with the flicker lights. Carl is taken by the centipede legs and pulled into flesh jelly dissolving bones—Thick black hair sprouts through his tumescent flesh—He falls through a maze of penny arcades and dirty pictures, locker rooms, barracks, and prison flesh empty with the colorless smell of death—

Cold metal excrement on all the walls and benches, silver sky raining the metal word fallout—Sex sweat like iron in the mouth. Scores are coming in. Pretend an interest.

In a puppet booth the manipulator takes pictures of bored insolent catatonics with eight-hour erections reading comics and chewing gum. The impresario is a bony Nordic with green fuzz on his chest and legs. "I get mine later with the pictures. I can't touch the performers. Wall of glass you know show you something interesting."

He pulls aside curtain: schoolboy room with a banner and pin-ups. on the bed naked boy puppet reading comics and chewing gum with a hypo.

Ghost your German. Spit penny arcades, tattoo booths, Nordic processions, human performers, trapeze artists. Whores of all sexes importune from scenic railways and ferris wheels where they rent cubicles, push up manhole covers in a puff of steam, pull at passing pant cuffs, careen out of the Tunnel of Love waving condoms of jissom. Old blind queens with dirty peep shows built into their eye sockets disguise themselves as penny arcades and feel for a young boy's throbbing cock with cold metal hands, sniff pensively at bicycle seats in Afghan Hound drag, Puerto Joselito is located through legs. Ghost slime sitting naked on tattoo booths, virus flesh of curse. suffocating town, this. Ways to bury explorer.

Old junky street cleaners push little red wagons sweeping up condoms and empty H caps, KY tubes, broken trusses and sex devices, kif garbage and confetti, moldy jockstraps and bloody Kotex, shit-stained color comics, dead kitten and afterbirths, jenshe babies of berdache and junky.

Everywhere the soft insidious voice of the Pitchman delayed action language lesson muttering under all your pillows "Shows all kinds masturbation and self-abuse. Young boys need it special."

Last Hints

CARL DESCENDED a spiral iron stairwell into a labyrinth of lockers, tier on tier of wire mesh and steel cubicles joined by catwalks and ladders and moving cable cars as far as he could see, tiers shifting interpenetrating swinging beams of construction, blue flare of torches on the intent young faces. locker room smell of moldy jock-straps, chlorine and burning metal, escalators and moving floors start stop change course, synchronize with balconies and perilous platforms eaten with rust. Ferris wheels silently penetrate the structure, roller coasters catapult through to the clear sky—a young workman walks the steel beams with the sun in his hair out of sight in a maze of catwalks and platforms where coffee fires smoke in rusty barrels and the workers blow on their black cotton gloves in the clear cold morning through to the sky beams with sun in his hair the workers blow on their cold morning, dropped down into the clicking turnstiles. buzzers, lights and stuttering torches smell of ozone. Breakage is constant. Whole tiers shift and crash in a yellow cloud of rust, spill boys masturbating on careening toilets, iron urinals trailing a wake of indecent exposure, old men in rocking chairs screaming antifluoride slogans, a Southern Senator sticks his fat frog face out of the outhouse and brays with inflexible authority: "And Ah advocates the extreme penalty in the worst form there is for anyone convicted of trafficking in, transporting, selling or caught in using the narcotic substance known as nutmeg. . . I wanna say further that ahm a true friend of the Nigra and understand all his simple wants. Why, I got a good Darkie in here now wiping my ass."

Wreckage and broken bodies litter the girders, slowly collected by old junkies pushing little red wagons patient and calm with gentle larcenous old woman fingers. gathering blue torch flares light the calm intent young worker faces.

Carl descended a spiral iron smell of ozone. Breakage is of lockers tier on tier crash in yellow cloud as far as he could see of indecent exposure on toilets. Swinging beams construct the intent young faces.

Locker room toilet on five levels seen from the ferris wheel. flash of white legs, shiny pubic hairs and lean brown arms, boys masturbating with soap under rusty showers form a serpent line beating on the lockers, vibrates through all the tiers and cubicles unguarded platforms and dead-end ladders dangling in space, workers straddling beams beat out runic tunes with shiny ball peen hammers. The universe shakes with metallic adolescent lust. The line disappears through a green door slide down to the subterranean baths twisting through torch flares the melodious boy-cries drift out of ventilators in all the locker rooms, barracks, schools and prisons of the world. "Joselito, Paco, Enrique."

Jacking off he is whiff stateroom that is always kept locked—and word dust dirtied his body falling through the space between worlds—

The third kif pipe he went through the urinal sick and dizzy. He just down from the country. He just down from the green place by the dog's mirror. Sometimes came to a place by the dogs. . . Jungle sounds and smells drift from his coat lapels. A lovely Sub that boy.

Ghosts of Panama clung to our bodies—"You come with me, Meester?"—On the boy's breath a flesh—His body slid from my hands in soap bubbles—We twisted slowly to the yellow sands, traced fossils of orgasm—

"You win something like jellyfish, Meester."

Under a ceiling fan, naked and sullen, stranger color through his eyes the lookout different—fading Panama photos swept out by an old junky coughing spitting in the sick dawn—

(phosphorescent metal excrement of the city—brain eating birds patrol the iron streets.)

Hospital smell of dawn powder—dead rainbow post

cards swept out by an old junky in backward countries.

"I don't know if you got my last hints as we shifted commissions, passing where the awning flaps from the Café de France—Hurry up—Perhaps Carl still has his magic lantern—Dark overtakes someone walking—I don't know exactly where you made this dream—Sending letter to a coffin is like posting it in last terrace of the garden—I would never have believed realms and frontiers of light exist—I'm so badly informed and totally green troops—B.B., hurry up please—"

(Stopped suddenly to show me a hideous leather body)—"I'm almost without medicine."

It was still good bye then against the window outside 1920's movie, flesh tracks broken—Sitting at a long table where the doctor couldn't reach and I said: "He has your voice and end of the line—Fading breath on bed showing symptoms of suffocation—I have tuned them out—How many plots have been forestalled before they could take shape in boy haunted by the iron claws?—Meanwhile a tape recorder cuts old newspapers." Panama clung to our bodies naked under the ceiling fan—excrement at the far end of forgotten streets—hospital smell on the dawn wind—

(Peeled his phosphorescent metal knees, brain broiled in carrion hunger.)

On the sea wall under fading Panama photo casual ghost of adolescent T-shirt traced fossil-like jellyfish—

"On the sea wall if you got my last hints over the tide flats—I don't know exactly where—woke up in other flesh—shirt with Chinese characters—breeze from the Café de France—lantern burning insect wings—I'm almost without medicine—far away—storms—crackling sounds—Nothing here now but the circling albatross—dead post card waiting a place forgotten—"

On the sea wall met a boy under the circling albatross—Peeled his red-and-white T-shirt to brown flesh and grey under like ash and passed a joint back and forth as we dropped each other's pants and he looked down face like Mayan limestone in the kerosene lamp sputter of burning insect wings over the tide flats—Woke up in other flesh the lookout different—hospital smell of backward countries—

Where the Awning Flaps

"So we got our rocks off permutating through each other's facilities on the blue route and after a little practice we could do it without the projector and perform any kinda awful sex act on any street corner behind the blue glass stirring the passing rectums and pubic hairs like dry leaves falling in the pissoir: "*J'aime ces types vicieux qu'ici montrent la bite—*"

Drinking from his eyes the idiot green boys plaintive as wind leaves erect wooden phallus on the graves of dying Lemur Peoples.

"Fluck flick take any place. Johnny you-me-neon-asshole-amigos-now."

"You only get a hard-on with my permission."

"Who you now Meester? Flick fluck take Johnny

over. Me screw Johnny up same asshole? You me make flick-fluck-one-piece?"

Just hula hoop through each other to idiot Mambo. Every citizen of the area has a blueprint like some are Electricals and some are Vegetable Walking Carbonics and so on, it's very technical. boy jissom tracks through rectal mucus and Johnny.

"One track out so: panels of shadow."

"Me finish Johnny night."

So we get our rectums in transparent facilities blue route process together. slow night to examine me. every dawn smell fingers the passing rectum. finger on all cocks: "I-you-me in the pissoir of present time." "Idiot fuck you-me-Johnny. "flick fluck idiot asshole buddies like a tree frog clinging in permission. Who are you green hands? Fungoid purple?"

"Johnny over. Me screw. Flick fluck one piece."

Warm spermy smell to idiot Mambo. Silence belches smell of ozone and rectal flight: "Here goes examiner other rectums naked in Panama. citizen of the area."

On the sea wall met the guide under the Circling Albatross. Peeled his red- and white-striped T-shirt to brown flesh and grey under like ash and we passed a joint back and forth as we dropped each other's pants and he looked down face like Mayan limestone in the kerosene lamp sputter of burning insect wings.

"I screw Johnny up ass." He jumped with his knees on the bed and slapped his thighs, cock-shadow pulsing on the blue paint wall. "*Así como peeeeerross.*" ass hairs spread over the tide flats. Woke up in other flesh, the lookout different, one boy naked in Panama dawn wind.

Casual adolescent of urinals and evening flesh gone when I woke up—Age flakes fall through the pissoir—Ran into my old friend Jones—so badly off—Forgotten coughing in 1920 movie—Vaudeville voices hustle on bed service—I nearly suffocated trying on the boy's breath—That's Panama—Brain-eating birds patrol the low frequency brain waves—nitrous flesh swept out by your voice and end of receiving set—Sad hand tuned out the stale urine of Panama.

"I am dying, Meester?—forgotten coughing in 1920 street?"

Genital pawn ticket peeled his stale underwear, shirt flapping whiffs of young hard-on—brief boy on screen laughing my skivvies all the way down—whispers of dark street in Puerto Assis—Meester smiles through the village wastrel—Orgasm siphoned back telegram: "Johnny pants down." (that stale summer dawn smell in the garage—vines twisting through steel—bare feet in dog's excrement—)

Panama clung to our bodies from Las Palmas to David on camphor sweet smell of cooking paregoric—Burned down the republic—The druggist no glot clom Fliday—Panama mirrors of 1910 under seal in any drugstore—He threw in the towel morning light on cold coffee stale breakfast table—little cat smile—pain and death smell of his sickness in the room with me—three souvenir shots of Panama City—Old friend came and stayed all day face eaten by "I need *more*"—I have noticed this in the New World—

"You come with me, Meester?"

And Joselito moved in at Las Playas during the essentials—Stuck in this place—iridescent lagoons, swamp delta, bubbles of coal gas still be saying "*A ver, Luckees*" a hundred years from now—A rotting teakwood balcony propped up Ecuador.

"Die Flowers and Jungle bouncing they can't city?"

On the sea wall two of them stood together waving—Age flakes coming down hard here—Hurry up—Another hollow ticket—Don't know if you got my last hints trying to break out of this numb dizziness with Chinese characters—I was saying over and over shifted commissions where the awning flaps in your voice—end of the line—Silence out there beyond the gate—casual adolescent shirt flapping in the evening wind—

"Old photographer trick wait for Johnny—Here goes Mexican cemetery."

On the sea wall met a boy with red- and white-striped T-shirt—(P.G. town in the purple twilight)—The boy peeled off his stale underwear scraping erection—warm rain on the iron roof—under the ceiling fan stood naked on bed service—bodies touched electric film—contact sparks tingled—fan whiffs of young hard-on washing adolescent T-shirt—The blood smells drowned voices and end of the line—That's Panama—sad movie drifting in islands of rubbish, black lagoons and fish people waiting a place forgotten

—fossil honky-tonk swept out by a ceiling fan—Old photographer trick tuned them out.

"I am dying, Meester?"

Flashes in front of my eyes naked and sullen—rotten dawn wind in sleep—death rot on Panama photo where the awning flaps.

Sad servant stood on the sea wall in sepia clouds of Panama.

"Boy I was washed face in Panama maybe undressed there. money. good bye."

Johnny Yen's last *adiós* out of focus.

1920 Movies

FILM UNION SUB spirit couldn't find the cobbled road content with an occasional Mexican in the afternoon a body sadness to say good bye smell of blood and excrement with the wind sad distant voices infer his absence as wind and dust in empty streets of Mexico.

"I am the Director. You have known me for a long time. Mister, leave cigarette money."

Iron cell wall painted flaking rust—Grifa smoke through the high grate window of blue night—Two prisoners sit on lower iron shelf bunk smoking. One is American the other Mexican—The Cell vibrates with silent blue motion of prison and all detention in time.

"Johnny I think you little bit *puto* queer."

"*Sí.*" Johnny held up thumb and finger an inch apart.

"I screw Johnny up ass? *Bueno* Johnny?" His fingers flicked Johnny's shirt. They stood up. José hung his shirt on a nail, Johnny passed shirt and José hung one shirt over the other. "*Ven acá.*" He caught Johnny's belt-end with one hand and flipped the belt-tongue out and opened fly buttons with pickpocket fingers.

"Johnny pants down. *Ya duro.* Johnny hard. I think like *mucho* be screwed."

"*Claro.*"

"Fuck Johnny, Johnny come too?"

José moved into the bunk on knees: "Like this Johnny," he slapped his thighs. "*Como perros.*"

He opened a tin of vaseline as the other moved into place and shoved a slow twisting finger up Johnny's ass.

"Johnny like?"

"*Mucho.*"

"Johnny flip now."

He held Johnny's thighs and moved his cock in slow.

"Breathe in deep Johnny."

His cock slid in as Johnny breathed in. They froze there breathing: "*Bueno,* Johnny?"

"*Bueno.*"

"*Vámanos.*" Shadow bodies twisted on the blue wall. "Johnny sure start now."

"You is coming Johnny?"

"*Siiiiii.*"

"Here goes Johnny." Spurts cross the surplus blanket smell of iron prison flesh and clogged toilets. pick-pocket finger on his balls squeezing the spurts, cock throbbing against his spine, he squeezed through a maze of penny arcades dirty pictures in the blue Mexican night. The two bodies fell languidly apart bare feet on the Army blanket. Grifa smoke blown down over black shiny pubic hairs copper and freckle flesh. Paco's cock came up in smoke.

"*Otra vez,* Johnny?" He put his hands behind Johnny's knees.

"Johnny hear knees now."

Mexican thighs: "*Como perros* I fuck you."

Walls painted blue smoke through the grate. Finger up Johnny's ass moved two prisoners. He held Johnny's thighs and vibrated silent deep Johnny. His cock slid: "Johnny, I in."

"Let's go," twisted the iron frame. "*Porqué no?*"

"*Bueno,* Johnny." Candle shadow bodies. "Johnny sure *desnudate por completo. . .* Johnny?"

"*Siiii?*"

"Here goes *completo.*" Plus blankets smell of iron and shirt on nail. Mexican pickpocket one shirt over the other. Spurts maze of dirty pictures. He pushed toe blue Mexican night Johnny pants down.

Part bare feet on the blanket. Black shiny pubic hairs.

"I think like *mucho* be José—Paco—Enrique."

"*Como perros* Johnny like? Breathe José in there deep Johnny."

His cock iron frame for what not breathing: "Let's go bunk."

"You is coming plus Paco." Cross blanket smell of

Johnny flicked one shirt. Go *completo* plus Kiki. He flipped the tongue street: "You is coming for Johnny."

One shirt spilling head. The bodies feel cock flip out and up.

"*Como eso* I fuck you." One shirt spilling Johnny. Finger on his balls. Cock flipped out and up. black shiny pubic head. the bodies smoke.

"Fuck on knees. Lie down blanket. *Como eso* through the iron." He feel tongue on knees. smoke fuck on knees.

"*Mucho* be *ángel como eso.*"

"Deep Johnny."

Shoved white knees. Vaseline finger vibrate thighs. "Flip now."

"Paco? slow."

"*Sí,* the ass Johnny? I screw Johnny up ass?"

Spurts prison flesh to Mexican night: "Vibrate, Johnny."

"I screw Johnny."

"Let's go."

"Johnny knees down. *Boca abajo.* You is coming *como eso?*"

"Hard bunk Johnny. Me up in Freckles. *Como perros* like on knees."

"I screw Johnny Mexican. Smoke fuck Johnny. *Como eso* Johnny fuck on knees."

He feel flipped the knees. "You is coming *otra vez* Johnny?" He flipped Johnny. vaseline finger see the ass. one shirt spilling Johnny flicked out and up.

"One *mucho* Johnny flip now."

"Breathe José into hilt ass Johnny."

"Start now."

"You is coming?"

Spurts cross *calzoncillos todo.* José hung his prison flesh. Finger on his balls feel "come here." He caught Johnny belt spine. He feel flipped the belt-tongue cross pickpocket fingers. The bodies fell languidly. Cock flipped out and up. Grifa smoke blown down line. "*A ver* like this." He clipped into the bunk on knees like: "*Como perros* come Johnny."

José knees. Vaseline finger twisting Johnny's thighs.

"Flip now. José slow deep Johnny." His cock slid ass Johnny.

"*Bueno* Johnny?"

Breathing: "Let's go bunk. Johnny candle shadow now."

"You is coming *por completo.*"

"*Siiii,*" spurts spilling cross pickpocket toe Mexican night cock flipped out and up. Part bare feet.

"Fuck on knees like" (Moving two prisoners in the blue? Is American bunk?)

"*Mucho* Johnny vibrate blue pressure. Breathe José in there. *Sí* iron frame."

"*Porqué no?*"

"Johnny here go *completo* plus Kiki." Hung his prison flesh on nail.

Johnny toilet finger on his balls feel other spurts cock. He fell flipped the pictures. The bodies fell street.

"*Claro* you like *mucho* be Kiki. *A ver. Como eso.*" Just

hula hoop through each other to idiot Mambo. . .all idiot Mambo spattered to control mechanization.

"Salt Chunk Mary" had all the "nos" and none of them ever meant "yes." She named a price heavy and cold as a cop's blackjack on a winter night and that was it. She didn't name another. Mary didn't like talk and she didn't like talkers. She received and did business in the kitchen. And she kept it in a sugar bowl. Nobody thought about that. Her cold grey eyes would have seen the thought and maybe something goes wrong on the next lay John Citizen come up with a load of 00 into your soft and tenders or Johnny Law just happens by. She sat there and heard. When you spread the gear out on her kitchen table she already knows where you sloped it. She looks at the gear and a price falls out heavy and cold and her mouth closes and stays shut. If she doesn't want to do business she just wraps the gear up and shoves it back across the table and that is that. Mary keeps a blue coffee pot and a pot of salt pork and beans always on the wood stove. When you fall in she gets up without a word and puts a mug of coffee and plate of salt chunk in front of you. You eat and then you talk business. Or maybe you take a room for a week to cool off. room 18 on the top floor I was sitting in the top room rose wall paper smoky sunset across the river. I was new in the game and like all young thieves thought I had a license to steal. It didn't last. Sitting there waiting on the Japanese girl works in the Chink laundry a soft knock and I open the door naked with a hard-on it was the top floor all the way up you understand nobody on that landing. "Ooooh" she says feeling it up to my oysters a drop of lubricant squeezed out and took the smoky sunset on rose wall paper I'd been sitting there naked thinking about what we were going to do in the rocking chair rocks off down the line she could get out of her dry goods faster than a junky can fix when his blood is right so we rocked away into the sunset across the river just before blast off that old knock on the door and I shoot this fear load like I never feel it wind up is her young brother at the door in his cop suit been watching through the key hole and learn about the birds and the bees some bee I was in those days good looking kid had all my teeth and she knew all the sex currents goose for pimple always made her entrance when your nuts are tight and aching a red haired smoky rose sunset one bare knee rubbing greasy pink wall paper he was naked with a hard-on waiting on the Mexican girl from Marty's a pearl of lubricant squeezed slowly out and glittered on the tip of his cock. There was a soft knock at the door. He got up off the crumpled bed and opened the door. The girl's brother stood there smiling. The red haired boy made a slight choking sound as blood rushed to his face pounded and sang in his ears. The young face there on the landing turned black around the edges. The red haired boy sagged against the door jamb. He came to on the bed the Mexican kid standing over him.

"All right now? Sis can't come."

The Mexican kid unbuttoned his shirt. He kicked

off his sandals dropped his pants and shorts grinning and his cock flipped out half up. The Mexican kid brought his finger up in three jerks and his cock came up with it nuts tight pubic hairs glistening black he sat down on the bed.

"Vaseline?"

The red haired boy pointed to the night table. He was lying on the bed breathing deeply his knees up. The Mexican kid took a jar of vaseline out of a drawer. He kneeled on the bed and put his hands behind the freckled knees and shoved the boy's knees up to his trembling red ears. He rubbed vaseline on the pink rectum with a slow circular pull. The red haired boy gasped and his rectum spread open. The Mexican kid slid his cock in. The two boys locked together breathing in each other's lungs. After the girl left I walk down to Marty's where I meet this Johnson has a disgruntled former chauffeur map indicates where a diamond necklace waits for me wall safe behind the Blue Period. Or maybe you Picasso on Rembrandt and cool off like I was sitting in a Turner sunset on the Japanese girl doing my simple artisan job hot and heavy. Mary she kept the guide ready her eyes heavy and cold as a cop's come around with the old birds and bees business. Nobody thought about that cold outside agent call. Recall John Citizen came up on her. Johnny Law just happens by magic shop in Westbourne Grove. Smell these conditions of ash? I twig that old knack. Klinker is dead. Blackout fell on these foreign suburbs here.

"Be careful of the old man. kinda special deputy carries a gun in the car."

Music fading in the East St. Louis night broken junk of exploded star sad servant of the inland side shirt flapping in a wind across the golf course a black silver sky of broken film precarious streets of yesterday back from shadows the boy solid now I could touch almost you know both of us use the copper luster basin in the blue attic room now Johnny's back. Who else put a slow cold hand on your shoulder shirt flapping shadows on a wall long ago fading streets a distant sky?

They walked through a city of black and white movies fading streets of thousand-run smoke faces. figures of the world slow down to catatonic limestone.

City blocks speed up out in photo flash. Hotel lobbies 1920 time fill with slow grey film fallout and funeral urns of Hollywood. Never learn? The guide clicked him through a silent turnstile into a cubicle of blue glass and mirrors so that any panel of the room was at alternate intervals synchronized with the client's sex-pulse mirror or wall of glass into the next cell on all sides and the arrangement was an elaborate permutation and very technical. . . So Johnny the Guide said: "The first clause in our blue contract is known as the examination to which both parties must submit. . . We call it the probing period, now isn't that cute?"

The guide put on helmet of photo goggles and antennae of orange neon flickering, smelling bat wings: "Johnny pants down. Johnny cock hard." He brought his arm up from the elbow swimming in for close-ups of Johnny's erection: take slow and take fast under flickering vowel colors: I red/U green/E white/O blue/A black/"Bend over Johnny." The examiner floats up from the floor, swims down through heavy water from the ceiling, shoots up from toilet bowl, English baths, underwater takes of genitals and pubic hairs in warm spermy water. The goggles lick over his body phosphorescent moths, through rectal hairs orange halos flicker around his penis. In his sleep, naked Panama nights, the camera pulsing in blue silence and ozone smells, sometimes the cubicle open out on all sides into purple space. X-ray photos of viscera and fecal movements, his body a transparent blue fish.

"So that's the examination we call it, sees all your processes. You can't deceive us in any way at all and now you got the right to examine me."

Lee put on the photo goggles melt in head and saw the guide now blond with brown eyes slender and tilted forward. He moved in for a close-up of the boy's flank and took his shirt off followed the pants down, circled the pubic hair forest in slow autogyros, zeroed in for the first stirrings of tumescence, swooping from the stiffening blood tube to the boy's face, sucking eyes with neon proboscis, licking testicles and rectum. The goggles and antennae fade in smoke and slow street-eyes swim up from grey dust and funeral urns. and in his sleep naked blue movies slow motion. Pulsing blue silence photos genitals and pubic hairs in rectal mucus and carbolic soap. Alternate mirror and screen guide put on goggles walked through grey-filled shadows that melted in his head. In time focus the natives. like flickering bat wings over faded thousand-run faces, hearing, smelling through them like: "Johnny cock hard." Slowdown to statues with catatonic erection slow falling through colors red green black. A hot spread: cheeks close-up. And felt over Johnny's body the slow float down from Hollywood. came to the hot Panama nights. They clicked in through a squat toilet with walls of blue glass and underwater shots of warm soapy spermy water smell. so felt the boy neon fingers on sex spots breathing through sponge rock penis-flesh and brown intestine jungles lined with flesh-eating vines and frantic parasites of the area. . .

Naked in the Panama night, rectal mucus and carbolic soap. A blue screen guide put on goggles. Pale panels of shadow melted his head on all sides into blue silent wings over the clock of fecal movement smelling through them like transparent.

"A hot spread examination we call it. Johnny's body can't deceive us in any way. Came to the hot Panama nights to examine me."

Clicked into his head of blue glass. Close-up neon finger over the scar-impressions learning the instrument panels, recording on the transparent flesh of present time. It is happening right now. Slow 1920 finger rubbing vaseline on the cobra lamps, flickering movie shadows into the blue void. pulling finger rolls a cuneiform cylinder. Lens eye drank the boy's jissom in yellow light.

"Now Meester we flick fluck I me you cut." The two film tracks ran through impression screen. one track flash on other cut out in dark until cut back: "Me finish Johnny's shit. . . Clom through Johnny. . ." Hear rectums merging in flicks and orgasm of mutual processes. and pulsed in and out of each other's body on slow gills of sleep in the naked Panama nights and bent over the washstand in East St. Louis junk-sick dawn. smell of carbolic soap and rectal mucus and train whistle wake of blue silence and piss through my cock "I-you-me-fuck-up-ass-all-same-time-four-eyes." phantom cleavage crude and rampant. Every citizen can now grow sex forms in his bidet: in the night of Talara felt his hard-on against my khaki pants as we shifted slots and I browned a strange Danish dog under the nudes of Sweden. Warm spermy smell, room of blue glass strung together on light-lines of jissom and shit, shared meals and belches, the shifting of testes and contractions of rectum, flick-fluck back and forth.

"Here goes Johnny. We fluck now first run": in blue silence saw the two one track out: blue. Each meet image coming round the other erection-fucked-self and came other shit both.

"We flick-fluck I-you-film-tracks through rectal mucus and carbolic soap. Cut out pale panels of shadow." blue silent bat wings over rectums blending in transparent erection. a hot shit and all process together.

"Johnny's body can't deceive us in other body. slow night to examine me." sick dawn smell of carbolic finger. close-up finger on all cocks.

"I-you-me fuck up neon blind fingers phantom cleavage of boy impressions Witch Board of Present Time."

The idiot green boys leaped on Johnny like tree frogs clinging to his chest with sucker paws fungoid gills and red mushroom penis pulsing to the sex waves from Johnny eyes. warm spermy smell, lamps and flicker movies strung together on a million fingers shared meals and belches and lens-eye drank jissom. contract of rectum flight: "Here goes Johnny. One flight out." Screen other rectum naked in Panama night.

Ghost of Panama clung to our throats, coughing and spitting on separate spasm, phosphorescent breath fades in fractured air—sick flesh strung together on a million fingers shared meals and belches—nothing here now but circling word dust—dead post card falling through space between worlds—this road in this sharp smell of carrion—

We twisted slowly to black lagoons, flower floats and gondolas—tentative crystal city iridescent in the dawn wind—(Adolescents ejaculate over the tide flats.)

In the blue windy morning masturbating a soiled idiot body of cold scar tissue—catatonic limestone hands folded over his yen—a friend of any boy structure cut by a species of mollusk—Street boys of the green gathered—slow bronze smiles from a land of grass without memory—cool casual little ghosts of adolescent spasm—metal excrement and crystal glooms of the fish city—under a purple twilight our clothes shredded mummy linen on obsidian floors—Panama clung to our bodies—

"You come with me, Meester?"

Northern lights flicker from his "Yes"—The rope is adjusted—Writhing in wind black hair bursts through his flesh—Great canines tear into his gums with exquisite toothache pleasure—The green cab boys go all the way on any line.

Green boys—idiot irresponsibles—rolling in warm delta ooze fuck in color flashes through green jelly flesh that quivers together merging and drawing back in a temple dance of colors. "Hot licks us all the way we are all one clear green substance like flexible amber changing color and consistency to accommodate any occasion."

"This bad place Meester. You crazy or something walk around alone. Where you go?" The guide: impersonal screen swept by color winds light up green red white blue. antennae ears of flexible metal cartilage crackle blue spark messages leaving smell of ozone in the shiny black pubic hairs that grow on the guide's pink skull. blood and nerves hard meat cleaver his whole body would scorn to carry a weapon. And Being inside was him and more. face cut by image-flak impersonal young pilot eyes riding light rays pulsing through his head.

"Fluck Johnny? Up ass?" He guided Carl with electric tingles in spine and sex hairs through clicking gates and turnstiles, escalators and cable cars in synchronized motion. Impersonal young pilot eyes riding the blue silence permutated Carl into an iron cubicle with painted blue walls pallet on the floor brass tea tray kif pipes and jars of phosphorescent green sex paste. wall over the pallet two-way mirrors opposite wall of glass opening on the next cubicle and so on, sex acts into the blue distance. The Guide pointed to the mirror: "We fuck good Johnny. On air now."

"Johnny pants down"—he was smearing the sex paste on "Johnny's" ass hot licking the white nerves and pearly genitals—Carl's lips and tongue swelled with blood and his face went phosphorescent penis purple—slow penetrating incandescent flesh tubes siphoned his body into a pulsing sphere of blue jelly floated over skeletons locked in limestone—The cubicles shifted—Carl was siphoned back through the Guide and landed with a fluid plop as the cubicles permutated fucking shadows through ceilings of legs and sex hairs, black spirals of phantom assholes lifting and twisting like a Panhandle cyclone.

UNIT I: WHITE: "You wanta screw me?" "I wanta screw you." Two marble white youths with identical erections stand on a white tile bathroom floor. The young faces sharp flash bulb of urgency fade-out stale empty of hunger. (Crystal flute music. The boys step from Attic frieze on Greek urns.)

Tarnished pub mirrors of the gentle ghost-people, grey faded clubs under yellowing tusks of the beast killed by improbable hyphenated names. In bath cubicles and locker rooms shut for the summer white light bent over a chair—

UNIT II: BLACK: "Bend over." As the white youth bends over turns brown then black. The other half drums on his back. The youths fade in obsidian mirror, smell of opium and copal.

UNIT III: GREEN: "Loosen you up a bit." Black finger dips into green jelly. The finger turns green in rusty limestone with a slow circular pull. green boy of flexible green amber, bright lizards and beetles incrusted here and there, twists sighs out in jungle sound of frogs and bird calls and howler monkeys like wind in the trees, slow movement of rivers and forests cross the Drenched Lands. Vines twist through the boys smell of mud flats where sting rays bask in shallow canals brown with excrement sewage delta and coal gas swamps under orange gas flares and grey metal fallout.

UNIT IV: RED: "Breathe in Johnny. Here goes." Red youths fuck bent over a brass bed in Mexico. feel through a maze of penny arcades and dirty pictures to the blue Mexican night. penis of different size, shape swell in and out flicker faces and bodies burning flesh sparks from camp fires and red fuck lights in blue cubicles.

UNIT V: BLUE: SILENCE. The two bodies merge in a blue sphere. Vapor trails cross a blue sky. Out on a blue wave high fi cool and blue as liquid air in our slate-blue houses wrapped in orange flesh-robes that grow on us.

UNIT I: WHITE: The boys slow down to phallic statues. They fade out in old photos and 1920 movies. hairs rub the exquisite toothache pleasure: "I wanta screw you." Flash bulb of urgency fade: "Loosen you up a bit." The finger turns green out in stale streets of cry.

UNIT III: GREEN: The green boy of green flute music. worn amber with lizards incrusted and finger rusty sighs out in the spectral smell of birdcalls and howler monkeys like gentle ghost-people. slow movement of brown rivers. The boys in speed-up and barracks toilet smell of the mud flats and the white youths fuck brown with excrement under a static red sky. smell of subway dawns and turnstile. tarnished pub mirrors jungle sound of frogs. army of trees killed by the improbable hyphenated name. tendril movement in white light.

UNIT V: BLUE: "The initiate awoke in other flesh the lookout different." Cool blue casual youth check Board Books of the world finger light and cold as Spring wind. Little high blue notes drift through slate-blue houses. Street gangs Uranian born in the face of appalling conditions. Fade-out in "Mr. Bradly Mr. Martin" down the flash funnel of copy faces out in summer dawn we made it in a smell of carbolic soap and rectal mucus. slow green tendrils through the hair and the purple fungoid gills breathe empty green house. plaintive monkey phallus on the grave of dying peoples. red mesas cut by a blue wind. Copper youths languidly masturbate, coming in puffs of blue smoke cross the translucent red stone buildings and copper domes of the city a white tooth sky cut with vapor trails. flash bulb of urgency train whistles fade in black finger and basement pot. cool blue light in stale streets of cry. In the hyacinths green boys of a green flute music sigh out birdcalls and howler monkey like: "You wanta screw me?" slow movement of rivers. the boy's unit green with shit smell of the mud flats. Jelly substance like excrement flares under static red sky. Like smell RED: "Breathe in Johnny. Here goes." Twisting over a brass bed in Mexico. The boys slow fucking shift old photos and 1910 movie of the two bodies. merge in blue smoke rings loosen you up out drift away slate-blue Northern sky water. limestone cave fades in blue drum of gentle ghost-people. draft youths with indentical erection in speed-up barracks orgasm. pub mirrors green fade movie club. under the faces improbable names. green boys formed the fuck drum message lights a blue flame inside phallus (boy ear, blue sky). The initiate awoke in the city of red stone different train whistle masturbate with fingers light as Spring smoke. cross road of the world the high blue domes of the city and blue children born in the face of white battle. bulb of urgency train war unit. Mr. Bradly cool blue down the flash funnel out in stale summer dawn smell. black drum talks mucus. The youths twist flowers and sewers of the world. drum puffs of paint flesh. "flesh diseased dirty pictures how long you want us to fuck very nice Mister? To cheat and betray us been sent?"

We got to untalking on question studying the porch noise home from work used to be me Mister diseased waiting face return various bits and pieces of the picture: that he coin a "nice-guy-myth" the bastard dirtier than Coin Smell Dorm.

"What you trying to unload on somebody Mister? radioactive garbage?"

Where You Belong

My trouble began when they decide I am executive timber—It starts like this: a big blond driller from Dallas picks me out of the labor pool to be his house-boy in a prefabricated air-conditioned bungalow—He comes on rugged but as soon as we strip down to the ball park over on his stomach kicking white wash and screams out "Fuck the shit out of me!"—I give him a slow pimp screwing and in solid—When this friend comes down from New York the driller says "This is the boy I was telling you about"—And friend looks me over slow chewing his cigar and says: "What are you doing over there with the apes? Why don't you come over here with the Board where you belong?" And he slips me a long slimy look Friend works for the

Trak News Agency—"We don't report the news—We write it." And next thing I know they have trapped a grey flannel suit on me and I am sent to this school in Washington to learn how this writing the news before it happens is done—I sus it is the Mayan Caper with an IBM machine and I don't want to be caught short in a grey flannel suit when the lid blows off—So I act in concert with the Subliminal Kid who is a technical sergeant and has a special way of talking. And he stands there a long time chewing tobacco is our middle name "—What are you doing over there?—Beat your mother to over here—Know what they mean if they start job for instance?—Open shirt, apparent sensory impressions calling slimy terms of the old fifty-fifty jazz—Kiss their target all over—Assembly points in Danny Deever—By now they are controlling shithouse of the world—Just feed in sad-eyed youths and the machine will process it —After that Minraud sky—Their eggs all over—These officers come gibbering into the queer bar don't even know what buttons to push—('Run with the apes? Why don't you come across the lawn?') And he gives me a long slimy responsible cum grey flannel suit and I am Danny Deever in drag writing 'the news is served, sir.' Hooded dead gibber: 'this is the Mayan Caper'—A fat cigar and a long white nightie—Nonpayment answer is simple as Board Room Reports rigged a thousand years—Set up excuse and the machine will process it—Moldy pawn ticket runs a thousand years chewing the same argument—I Sekuin perfected that art along the Tang Dynasty—To put it another way IBM machine controls thought feeling and *apparent* sensory impressions—Subliminal lark—These officers don't even know what buttons to push—Whatever you feed into the machine on subliminal level the machine will process—So we feed in 'dismantle thyself' and authority emaciated down to answer Mr of the Account in Ewyork, Onolulu, Aris, Ome, Oston—Might be just what I am look"—

We fold writers of all time in together and record radio programs, movie sound tracks, TV and juke box songs all the words of the world stirring around in a cement mixer and pour in the resistance message "Calling partisans of all nation—Cut word lines—Shift linguals—Free doorways—Vibrate 'tourists'—Word falling—Photo falling—Break through in Grey Room."

So the District Supervisor calls me in and puts the old white smaltz down on me:

"Now kid what are you doing over there with the niggers and the apes? Why don't you straighten out and act like a white man?—After all they're only human cattle—You know that yourself—Hate to see a bright young man fuck up and get off on the wrong track—Sure it happens to all of us one time or another—Why the man who went on to invent Shitola was sitting right where you're sitting now twenty-five years ago and I was saying the same things to him—Well he straightened out the way you're going to straighten out—Yes sir that Shitola combined with an ape diet—All we have to do is press the button and a hundred million more or less gooks flush down the drain in green cancer piss—

That's *big* isn't it?—And any man with white blood in him wants to be part of something big—You can't deny your blood kid—You're *white white white*—And you can't walk out on Trak—There's just no place to go."

Most distasteful thing I ever stood still for—Enough to make a girl crack her calories—So I walk out and the lid blew off—

Uranian Willy

URANIAN WILLY the Heavy Metal Kid, also known as Willy the Rat—He wised up the marks.

"This is war to extermination—Fight cell by cell through bodies and mind screens of the earth—Souls rotten from the Orgasm Drug—Flesh shuddering from the Ovens—Prisoners of the earth, come out—Storm the studio."

His plan called for total exposure—Wise up all the marks everywhere Show them the rigged wheel—Storm the Reality Studio and retake the universe—The plan shifted and reformed as reports came in from his electric patrols sniffing quivering down streets of the earth—the reality film giving and buckling like a bulkhead under pressure—burned metal smell of interplanetary war in the raw noon streets swept by screaming glass blizzards of enemy flak.

"Photo falling—Word falling—Use partisans of all nations—Target Orgasm Ray Installations—Gothenburg Sweden—Coordinates 8 2 7 6—Take Studio—Take Board Books—Take Death Dwarfs—Towers, open fire."

Pilot K9 caught the syndicate killer image on a penny arcade screen and held it in his sight—Now he was behind it in it was it—The image disintegrated in photo flash of total recognition—Other image on screen—Hold in sight—Smell of burning metal in his head—"Pilot K9, you are cut off—Back—Back—Back before the whole fucking shithouse goes up—Return to base immediately—Ride music beam back to base—Stay out of that time flak—All pilots ride Pan Pipes back to base."

It was impossible to estimate the damage—Board Books destroyed—Enemy personnel decimated—The message of total resistance on short wave of the world.

"Calling partisans of all nations—Shift linguals—Cut word lines—Vibrate tourists—Free doorways—Photo falling—Word falling—Break through in Grey Room."

Gongs of Violence

THE WAR BETWEEN the sexes split the planet into armed camps right down the middle line divides one thing from the other—And I have seen them all: The Lesbian colonels in tight green uniforms, the young aides and directives regarding the Sex Enemy from proliferating departments.

On the line is the Baby and Semen Market where the sexes meet to exchange the basic commodity which is known as the "property"—Unborn properties are shown with a time projector. As a clear young going face flashes on the auction screen frantic queens of all nations scream: "A doll! A doll! A doll!" And tear each other to pieces with leopard claws and broken bottles—tobacco auction sound effects—Riots erupt like sandstorms spraying the market with severed limbs and bouncing heads.

Biological parents in most cases are not owners of the property. They act under orders of absentee proprietors to install the indicated stops that punctuate the written life script—With each Property goes a life script—Shuttling between property farmers and script writers, a legion of runners, fixers, guides, agents, brokers, faces insane with purpose, mistakes and confusion pandemic—Like a buyer has a first-class Property and a lousy grade B life script.

"Fuck my life script will you you cheap downgrade bitch!"

Everywhere claim-jumpers and time-nappers jerk the time position of a property.

"And left me standing there without a 'spare jacket' or a 'greyhound' to travel in, my property back in 1910 Panama—I don't even feel like a human without my property—How can I feel without fingers?"

The property can also be jerked forward in time and sold at any age—The life of advanced property is difficult to say the least: poison virus agents trooping in and out at all hours: "We just dropped in to see some friends a population of patrols"—Strangers from Peoria waving quit claim deeds, skip tracers, collectors, claim-jumpers demanding payment for alleged services say: "We own the other half of the property."

"I dunno, me—Only work here—Technical Sergeant."

"Have you seen Slotless City?"

Red mesas cut by time winds—A network of bridges,

ladders, catwalks, cable cars, escalators and ferris wheels down into the blue depths—The precarious occupants in this place without phantom guards live in iron cubicles—constant motion on tracks, gates click open shut—buzzes, blue sparks, and constant breakage —(Whole squares and tiers of the city plunge into the bottomless void)—Swinging beams of construction and blue flares on the calm intent young worker faces—People rain on the city in homemade gliders and rockets —Balloons drift down out of faded violet photos—The city is reached overland by a series of trails cut in stone, suspension bridges and ladders intricately booby-trapped, wrong maps, disappearing guides—(A falling bureaucrat in blue glasses screams by with a flash of tin: "*Soy de la policia, señores—Tengo conexiónes*) hammocks, swings, balconies over the void—chemical gardens in rusty troughs—flowers and seeds and mist settle down from high jungle above the city—Fights erupt like sandstorms, through iron streets a wake of shattered bodies, heads bouncing into the void, hands clutching bank notes from gambling fights—Priests shriek for human sacrifices, gather partisans to initiate unspeakable rites until they are destroyed by counter pressures—Vigilantes of every purpose hang anyone they can overpower—Workers attack the passer-by with torches and air hammers—They reach up out of man-holes and drag the walkers down with iron claws—Rioters of all nations storm the city in a landslide of flame-throwers and Molotov cocktails—Sentries posted everywhere in towers open fire on the crowds at arbitrary intervals—The police never mesh with present time, their investigation far removed from the city always before or after the fact erupt into any café and machine-gun the patrons—The city pulses with slotless purpose lunatics killing from behind the wall of glass—A moment's hesitation brings a swarm of con men, guides, whores, mooches, script writers, runners, fixers cruising and snapping like aroused sharks—

(The subway sweeps by with a black blast of iron.)

The Market is guarded by Mongolian Archers right in the middle line between sex pressures jetting a hate wave that disintegrates violators in a flash of light—Everywhere posted on walls and towers in hovering autogyros these awful archers only get relief from the pressure by blasting a violator—Screen eyes vibrate through the city like electric dogs sniffing for violations—

Remind the Board of the unsavory case of "Black Paul" who bought babies with centipede jissom—When the fraud came to light a whole centipede issue was in the public streets and every citizen went armed with a flame-thrower—So the case of Black Paul shows what happens when all sense of civic responsibility breaks down—

It was a transitional period because of the Synthetics and everybody was raising some kinda awful life form in his bidet to fight the Sex Enemy—The results were not in all respects reasonable men, but the Synthetics were rolling off that line and we were getting some damned interesting types by golly blue heavy metal boys with near zero metabolism that shit once a century and then it's a slag heap and disposal problem in the worst form there is: sewage delta to a painted sky under orange gas flares, islands of garbage where green boy-girls tend human heads in chemical gardens, terminal cities under the metal word fallout like cold melted solder on walls and streets, sputtering cripples with phosphorescent metal stumps—So we decided the blue heavy metal boys were not in all respects a good blueprint.

I have seen them all—A unit yet of mammals and vegetables that subsist each on the shit of the other in prestidigital symbiosis and achieved a stage where one group shit out nothing but pure carbon dioxide which the other unit breathed in to shit out oxygen—It's the only way to live—You understand they had this highly developed culture with life forms between insect and vegetable, hanging vines, stinging sex hairs—The whole deal was finally relegated to It-Never-Happened-Department.

"Retroactive amnesia it out of every fucking mind screen in the area if we have to—How long you want to bat this tired old act around? A centipede issue in the street, unusual beings dormant in cancer, hierarchical shit-eating units—Now by all your stupid Gods at once let's not get this show on the road let's stop it."

Posted everywhere on street corners the idiot irresponsibles twitter supersonic approval, repeating slogans, giggling, dancing, masturbating out windows, making machine-gun noises and police whistles "And you, Dead Hand, stretching the Vegetable People come out of that compost heap—You are not taking your old fibrous roots past this inspector."

And the idiot irresponsibles scream posted everywhere in chorus: "Chemical gardens in rusty shit peoples!!"

"All out of time and into space. Come out of the timeword 'the' forever. Come out of the body word 'thee' forever. There is nothing to fear. There is no thing in space. There is no word to fear. There is no word in space."

And the idiot irresponsibles scream: "Come out of your stupid body you nameless assholes!!"

And there were those who thought A.J. lost dignity through the idiotic behavior of these properties but he said:

"That's the way I like to see them. No fallout. What good ever came from thinking? Just look there" (another heavy metal boy sank through the earth's crust and we got some good pictures. . .) "one of Shaffer's blueprints. I sounded a word of warning."

His idiot irresponsibles twittered and giggled and masturbated over him from little swings and snapped bits of food from his plate screaming: "Blue people NG conditions! Typical sight leak out!"

"All out of time and into space."

"Hello, Ima Johnny. the naked astronaut."

And the idiot irresponsibles rush in with space-suits and masturbating rockets spatter the city with jissom.

"Do not be alarmed citizens of Annexia—Report to

your Nearie Pro Station for chlorophyll processing—We are converting to vegetable state—Emergency measure to counter the heavy metal peril—Go to your 'Nearie'—You will meet a cool, competent person who will dope out all your fears in photosynthesis—Calling all citizens of Annexia—Report to Green Sign for processing."

"Citizens of Gravity we are converting all out to Heavy Metal. Carbonic Plague of the Vegetable People threatens our Heavy Metal State. Report to your nearest Plating Station. It's fun to be plated," says this well-known radio and TV personality who is now engraved forever in gags of metal. "Do not believe the calumny that our metal fallout will turn the planet into a slag heap. And in any case, is that worse than a compost heap? Heavy Metal is our program and we are prepared to sink through it. . ."

The cold heavy fluid settled in his spine 70 tons per square inch—Cool blocks of SOS—(Solid Blue Silence)—under heavy time—Can anything be done to metal people of Uranus?—Heavy his answer in monotone disaster stock: "Nobody can kick an SOS habit—70 tons per square inch—The crust from the beginning you understand—Tortured metal Ozz of earthquakes is tons focus of this junk"—Sudden young energy—I got up and danced—Know eventually be relieved—That's all I need—I got up and danced the disasters—"

Gongs of violence and how—Show you something—Berserk machine—"Shift cut tangle word lines—Word falling—Photo falling—"

"I said the Chief of Police skinned alive in Bagdad not Washington, D.C."

"Switzerland freezes all foreign assets."

"*Foreign assets?*"

"What?—British Prime Minister assassinated in Rightist coup?"

"Mindless idiot you have liquidated the Commissar."

"Terminal electric voice of C—All ling door out of agitated—Ta ta Stalin—Carriage age ta—"

Spectators scream through the track—The electronic brain shivers in blue and pink and chlorophyll orgasms spitting out money printed on rolls of toilet paper, condoms full of ice cream, Kotex hamburgers—Police files of the world spurt out in a blast of bone meal, garden tools and barbecue sets whistle through the air, skewer the spectators—crumpled cloth bodies through dead nitrous streets of an old film set—grey luminous flakes falling softly on Ewyork, Onolulu, Aris, Ome, Oston—From siren towers the twanging tones of fear—Pan God of Panic piping blue notes through empty streets as the berserk time machine twisted a tornado of years and centuries—Wind through dusty offices and archives—Board Books scattered to rubbish heaps of the earth—Symbol books of the all-powerful board that had controlled thought feeling and movement of a planet from birth to death with iron claws of pain and pleasure—The whole structure of reality went up in silent explosions—Paper moon and muslin trees and in the black silver sky great rents as the cover of the world rained down—Biologic film went up. . . "raining dinosaurs" "It sometimes happens. . .just an old showman" Death takes over the game so many actors buildings and stars laid flat pieces of finance over the golf course summer afternoons bare feet waiting for rain smell of sickness in the room Switzerland Panama machine guns in Bagdad rising from the typewriter pieces of finance on the evening wind tin shares Buenos Aires Mr. Martin smiles old names waiting sad old tune haunted the last human attic.

Outside a 1920 movie theater in East St. Louis I met Johnny Yen—His face showed strata of healed and half-healed fight scars—Standing there under the luminous film flakes he said: "I am going to look for a room in a good naborhood"—Captain Clark welcomes you aboard this languid paradise of dreamy skies and firefly evenings music across the golf course echoes from high cool corners of the dining room a little breeze stirs candles on the table. It was an April afternoon. After a while some news boy told him the war was over sadness in his eyes trees filtering light on dappled grass the lake like bits of silver paper in a wind across the golf course fading streets a distant sky.

WAS WEIGHTLESS—NEW YORK HERALD TRIBUNE PARIS APRIL 17, 1961—"One's arms and legs in and out through the crowd weigh nothing—Grey dust of broom in old cabin—Mr. Bradly Mr. I Myself sit in the chair as I subways and basements did before that—But hung in dust and pain wind—My hand writing leaning to a boy's grey flannel pants did not change although vapor trails fading in hand does not weigh anything now—Gagarin said grey junk yesterdays trailing the earth was quite plain and past the American he could easily see the shores of continents—islands and great rivers."

"Captain Clark welcomes you aboard."

Dead Fingers Talk

GLAD TO HAVE you aboard reader, but remember there is only one captain of this subway—Do not thrust your cock out the train window or beckon lewdly with thy piles nor flush thy beat benny down the drain—(Benny is overcoat in antiquated Times Square argot)—It is forbidden to use the signal rope for frivolous hangings or to burn Nigras in the washroom before the other passengers have made their toilet—

Do not offend the office manager—He is subject to take back the keys of the shithouse—Always keep it locked so no sinister stranger sneak a shit and give all the kids in the office some horrible condition—And Mr. Anker from accounting, his arms scarred like a junky from countless Wassermans, sprays plastic over it before he travails there—I stand on the Fifth Amendment, will not answer the question of the Senator from Wisconsin: "Are you or have you ever been a member of the male sex?"—They can't make Dicky whimper on the boys—Know how I take care of crooners?—Just listen to them—A word to the wise guy—I mean you gotta be careful of politics these days—Some old department get physical with you, kick him right in his coordinator—"Come see me tonight in my apartment under the school privy—Show you something interesting," said the janitor drooling green coca juice—

The city mutters in the distance pestilent breath of the cancerous librarian faint and intermittent on the warm Spring wind—

"Split is the wastings of the cup—Take it away," he said irritably—Black rocks and brown lagoons invade the world—There stands the deserted transmitter—Crystal tubes click on the message of retreat from the human hill and giant centipedes crawl in the ruined cities of our long home—Thermodynamics has won at a crawl—

"We were caught with our pants down," admits General Patterson. "They reamed the shit out of us."

Safest way to avoid these horrid perils is come over here and shack up with Scylla—Treat you right, kid—Candy and cigarettes—

Woke up in a Turkish Bath under a Johannesburg bidonville—

"Where am I you black bastards?"

"Why you junky white trash rim a shitting Nigger for an eyecup of paregoric?"

Dead bird—quail in the slipper—money in the bank —Past port and petal crowned with calm leaves she stands there across the river and under the trees—

Brains spilled in the cocktail lounge—The fat *macho* has burned down the Jai Lai bookie with his obsidian-handled .45—Shattering bloody blue of Mexico—Heart in the sun—Pantless corpses hang from telephone poles along the road to Monterrey—

Death rows the boy like sleeping marble down the Grand Canal out into a vast lagoon of souvenir post cards and bronze baby shoes—

"Just build a privy over me, boys," says the rustler to his bunk mates, and the sheriff nods in dark understanding Druid blood stirring in the winds of Panhandle—

Decayed corseted tenor sings Danny Deever in drag:

They have taken all his buttons off and cut his pants away

For he browned the colonel sleeping the man's ass is all agley

And he'll swing in 'arf a minute for sneaking shooting fey.

"Billy Budd must hang—All hands after to witness this exhibit."

Billy Budd gives up the ghost with a loud fart and the sail is rent from top to bottom—and the petty officers fall back confounded—"Billy" is a transvestite liz.

"There'll be a spot of bother about this," mutters The Master at Arms—The tars scream with rage at the cheating profile in the rising sun—

"Is she dead?"

"So who cares."

"Are we going to stand still for this?—The officers pull the switch on us," says young Hassan, ship's uncle—

"Gentlemen," says Captain Verre "I can not find words to castigate this foul and unnatural act whereby a boy's mother take over his body and infiltrate her horrible old substance right onto a decent boat and with bare tits hanging out, unfurls the nastiest colors of the spectroscope."

A hard-faced matron bandages the cunt of Radiant Jade—

"You see, dearie, the shock when your neck breaks has like an awful effect—You're already dead of course or at least unconscious or at least stunned—but—uh—well —you see—It's a *medical fact*—All your female insides is subject to spurt out your cunt the way it turned the last doctor to stone and we sold the results to Paraguay as a state of Bolivar."

"I have come to ascertain death not perform a hysterectomy," snapped the old auntie croaker munching a soggy crumpet with his grey teeth—A hanged man plummets through the ceiling of Lord Rivington's smart mews flat—Rivington rings the Home Secretary:

"I'd like to report a leak—"

"Everything is leaking—Can't stem it—*Sauve qui peut,*" snaps the Home Secretary and flees the country disguised as an eccentric Lesbian abolitionist—

"We hear it was the other way around, doc," said the snide reporter with narrow shoulders and bad teeth—

The doctor's face crimsoned: "I wish to state that I have been acting physician at Dankmoor prison for thirty years man boy and bestial and always keep my nose clean—Never compromise myself to be alone with the hanged man—Always insist on the presence of my baboon assistant witness and staunch friend in any position."

Mr. Gilly looks for his brindle-faced cow across the piney woods where armadillos, innocent of a cortex, frolic under the .22 of black Stetson and pale blue eyes.

"Lawd Lawd have you seen my brindle-faced cow?—Guess I'm taking up too much of your time—Must be busy doing *something* feller say—Good stand you got whatever it is—Maybe I'm asking too many questions—talking too much—You wouldn't have a rope would you?—A *hemp* rope? Don't know how I'd hold that old brindle-faced cow without a rope if I did come on her—"

Phantom riders—chili joints—saloons and the quick draw—hangings from horseback to the jeers of sporting women—black smoke on the hip in the Chink laundry—"No tickee no washee—Clom Fliday—"

Walking through the piney woods in the summer

dawn, chiggers pinpoint the boy's groin with red dots—Smell of boy balls and iron cool in the mouth—

"Now I want you boys to wear shorts," said the sheriff, "Decent women with telescopes can see you—"

Whiff of dried jissom in a bandanna rises from the hotel drawer—Sweet young breath through the teeth, stomach hard as marble spurts it out in soft, white globs—Funny how a man comes back to something he left in a Peoria hotel drawer 1929—

1920 tunes drift into the locker room where two boys first time tea high jack off to "My Blue Heaven"—

In the attic of the big store on bolts of cloth we made it—

"Careful—don't spill—Don't rat on the boys."

The cellar is full of light—In two weeks the tadpoles hatch—I wonder whatever happened to Otto's boy who played the violin? A hard-faced boy patch over one eye parrot on shoulder says: "Dead men tell no tales or do they?"—He prods the skull with his cutlass and a crab scuttles out—The boy reaches down and picks up a scroll of hieroglyphs—"The map!—The map!"

The map turns to shitty toilet paper in his hands, blows across a vacant lot in East St. Louis.

The boy pulls off the patch—The parrot flies away into the jungle—Cutlass turns to a machete—He is studying the map and swatting sand flies—

Junk yacks at our heels and predated checks bounce all around us in the Mayan ball court—

"Order in the court—You are accused of soliciting

with prehensile piles—What have you to say in your defense?"

"Just cooling them off, judge—Raw and bleeding—Wouldn't you?"

"I want you to *smell* this bar stool," said the paranoid ex-Communist to the manic FBI agent—"Stink juice, and you may quote me has been applied by paid hood-lums constipated with Moscow goldwasser."

The man in a green suit—old English cut with two side vents and change pockets outside—will swindle the aging proprietress of a florist shop—"Old flub got a yen on for me—"

Carnival of splintered pink peppermint—"Oh Those Golden Slippers"—He sits up and looks into a cobra lamp—

"I am the Egyptian," he said looking all flat and silly.

And I said: "Really, Bradford, don't be tiresome—"

Under the limestone cave I met a man with Medusa's head in a hatbox and said "Be careful" to the customs inspector, freezed his hand forever an inch from the false bottom—

Will the gentle reader get up off his limestones and pick up the phone?—Cause of death: completely un-interesting.

They cowboyed him in the steam room—Is this Cherry Ass Gio? The Towel Boy or Mother Gillig Old Auntie of Westminster Place? Only dead fingers talk in braille—

Second run cotton trace the bones of a fix—

But is all back seat dreaming since the hitchhiker

with the chewed thumb and he said: "If decided?—Could I ride with you chaps?"—(Heard about the death later in a Copenhagen bar—Told a story about crayfish and chased it with a Jew joke out behind the fear of what I tell him we all know here.) So it jumped in my throat and was all there like and ready when we were sitting under the pretties, star pretties you understand, not like me talking at all I used to talk differently. Who did?—Paris?

"Mr. Bradly Mr. Martin, Johnny Yenshe, Yves Martin."

Martin he calls himself but once in the London YMCA on Tottenham Court (never made out there)—Once on Dean Street in Soho—No it wasn't Dean Street that was someone else looked like Bradly—It was on some back time street, silent pockets of Mexico City—(half orange with red pepper in the sun)—and the weakness hit me and I leaned against a wall and the white spot never washed out of my glen plaid coat—Carried that wall with me to a town in Ecuador can't remember the name, remember the towns all around but not that one where time slipped on the beach—sand winds across the blood—half a cup of water and Martin looked at the guide or was it the other, the Aussie, the Canadian, the South African who is sometimes there when the water is given out and always there when the water gives out—and gave him half his own water ration with gambler fingers could switch water if he wanted to—On the street once Cavesbury Close I think it was somebody called him Uncle Charles in English and he didn't want to know the man walked away dragging one leg—

Mr. Bradly Mr. Martin, slotless fade-out of distant fingers in the sick morning—I told him you on tracks—couldn't reach me with the knife—couldn't switch iron—and zero time to stop—couldn't make turnstile—bad shape from death Mr. Shannon no cept pay of distant fingers spilling old photo—at me with the knife and fell over the white subway—on tracks I told—The shallow water came in with the tide of washed condoms and sick sharks fed on sewage—only food for this village—swamp delta to the green sky that does not change—I—We—They—sit quietly where you made this dream—"*Finnies nous attendons une bonne chance*"—(Footnote: Last words in the diary of Yves Martin who presumably died of thirst in the Egyptian desert with three companions—Just who died is uncertain since one member of the party has not been found alive or dead and identity of the missing person is dubious—The bodies were decomposed when found, and identification was based on documents. But it seems the party was given to exchange of identifications, and even to writing in each others' diaries—Other members of the expedition were Mr. Shannon, Mr. Armstrong, Monsieur Pillou, Ahmed Akid the guide—)

As the series is soon ending are these experiments really necessary?

Cross the Wounded Galaxies

THE PENNY ARCADE peep show long process in different forms.

In the pass the muttering sickness leaped into our throats, coughing and spitting in the silver morning. frost on our bones. Most of the ape forms died there on the treeless slopes. dumb animal eyes on "me" brought the sickness from white time caves frozen in my throat to hatch in the warm steamlands spitting song of scarlet bursts in egg flesh. beyond the pass, limestone slopes down into a high green savanna and the grass-wind on our genitals. came to a swamp fed by hot springs and mountain ice. and fell in flesh heaps. sick apes spitting blood laugh. sound bubbling in throats torn with the talk sickness. faces and bodies covered with pus foam. animal hair thru the purple sex-flesh. sick sound twisted thru body. underwater music bubbling in blood beds. human faces tentative flicker in and out of focus. We waded into the warm mud-water. hair and ape flesh off in screaming strips. stood naked human bodies covered with phosphorescent green jelly. soft tentative flesh cut with ape wounds. peeling other genitals. fingers and tongues rubbing off the jelly-cover. body melting pleasure-sounds in the warm mud. till the sun went and a blue wind of silence touched human faces and hair. When we came out of the mud we had names.

In the pass muttering arctic flowers. gusts of frost wind. bones and most of the ape still felt. invisible slopes. spitting the bloodbends human bones out of focus. and ape-flesh naked human body. Caves frozen in my throat. green jelly genitals. Limestone slopes cover our bodies melting in savanna and grass mud. shit and sperm fed hot till the sun went. The mountain touched human bubbling throats. Torn we crawled out of the mud. faces and bodies covered the purple sex-flesh. and the sickness leaped into our body underwater music bubble in the silver morning frost. faces tentative flicker in ape forms. into the warm mud and water slopes. cold screaming sickness from white time. covered with phosphorescent shed in the warm lands. spitting ape wounds. feeling egg flesh. green pleasure-sounds warm our genitals. blue wind of silence. Apes spitting sound faces thru pus foam. the talking sickness had names. The sound stood naked in the grass. music bubbling in the blood, quivering frog eggs and sound thru our throats and swap we had names for each other. tentative flicker-laugh and laughing washed the hairs off. down to his genitals. Human our bodies melted into when we crawled out.

And the other did not want to touch me because of the white worm-thing inside but no one could refuse if I wanted and ate the fear-softness in other men. The cold was around us in our bones. And I could see the time before the thing when there was green around and the green taste in my mouth and the green plant-shit on my legs. before the cold. . . And some did not eat flesh and died because they could not live with the thing inside. . . Once we caught one of the hairy men with our vine nets and tied him over a slow fire and left him there until he died and the thing sucked his screams moving in my face like smoke and no one could eat the flesh-fear of the hairy man and there was a smell in the cave bent us over. . . We moved to keep out of our excrement where white worms twisted up feeling for us and the white worm-sickness in all our bodies. We took our pots and spears and moved South and left the black flesh there in the ashes. . . Came to the great dry plain and only those lived who learned to let the thing surface and eat animal excrement in the brown water holes. . . Then thick grass and trees and animals. I pulled the skin over my head and I made another man put on the skin and horns and we fucked like the animals stuck together and we found the animals stuck together and killed both so I knew the thing inside me would always find animals to feed my mouth meat. . . Saw animals chase us with spears and woke eating my own hand and the blood in my mouth made me spit up a bitter green juice. But the next day I ate flesh again and every night we put on animal skins and smeared green animal excrement down our legs and fucked each other with whimpering snorting noises and stuck together shadows on the cave walls, and ate surface men. . . the skin over my head and green taste and the horns and we fucked before the thing inside me would. We caught one of the hairy men animaled him over a slow fire eating my own hand, the thing sucked his screams green bitter juice. Those lived who learned to let the softness in, eat animal excrement in the brown bones. . . I made another man put on the skin green plant shit on animal stuck together flesh. So I knew with the thing inside always find animals to feed with our vine nets. Blood in my mouth made me spit up moving in my face like the next day I ate flesh again. . . Moved to knee legs and fucked each other twisted up feeling and stuck together shadows on our bodies.

Glass blizzards thru the rusty limestone streets exploded flesh from the laughing bones. spattering blood cross urine of walls. We lived in sewers of the city, crab parasites in our genitals rubbing our diseased flesh thru each other on a long string of rectal mucus. place of the tapeworms with white bone faces and disk mouths feeling for the soft host mucus. the years. the long. the many. such a place. In a land of grass without memory, only food of the hordes moving south, the dark armadillo flesh killed in the cool morning grass with throwing sticks. The women and their thing police ate the flesh and we fought over their shit-encrusted pieces of armadillo gristle.

Glass blizzards without memory. only food of flesh was the dank urine of the city. crab parasites ate the flesh. thru jungles of breath when we copulate with white bones faces. place of nettles and scorpions for the soft host mucus. intestines sprouting weed room in the cool morning walls. the women in our genitals and bowels. fought over their shit, rubbing our diseased flesh-meat a mucus string: clawing thru shit place of tapeworms in some disk mouth. larval bodies feeling the penalty. the years. the long. the many. such shoots growing.

Sitting naked at the bottom of a well. the cool mud of evening touched our rectums. We shared a piece of armadillo gristle, eating it out of each other's mouths. above us a dry husk of insect bodies along the stone well wall and thistles over the well mouth against green evening sky. licking the gristle from his laughing teeth and gums I said: "I am Allah. I made you." A blue mist filled the well and shut off our word-breath. My hands sank into his body. We fell asleep in other flesh. Smells on our stomach and hands. Woke in noon sun, thistle shades cutting our soft night flesh.

Evening touched our rectums. mud shells and frogs croaking. licking the gristle asleep with other flesh. the cool mud of breath, and our bodies we shared.

branches in the wind. his knees. other mouths. against the green evening sky. "We laughing teeth and gums," I said. Hands woke in the noon sun soft night flesh. smell on our stomach. thistle shades cutting. penny arcade peep show—long process in different forms—dead fingers talk in braille.

Think Police keep all Board Room Reports—and we are not allowed to proffer the Disaster Accounts—Wind hand caught in the door—Explosive Bio-Advance Men out of space to employ Electrician in gasoline crack of history—Last of the gallant heroes—"I'm you on tracks, Mr. Bradly Mr. Martin"—Couldn't reach flesh in his switch—and zero time to the sick tracks—A long time between suns I held the stale overcoat—sliding between light and shadow—muttering in the dogs of unfamiliar score—cross the wounded galaxies we intersect, poison of dead sun in your brain slowly fading—Migrants of ape in gasoline crack of history, explosive bio-advance out of space to neon—"I'm you, Wind Hand caught in the door"—Coulnd't reach flesh—In sun I held the stale overcoat, Dead Hand stretching the throat—Last to proffer the disaster account on tracks. "See Mr. Bradly Mr.—"

And being blind may not refuse to hear: "Mr. Bradly Mr. Martin, disaster to my blood whom I created"—(The shallow water came in with the tide and the Swedish River of Gothenburg.)